Shadowfruit

By Gary Hewitt

Chapter 1 A Friendly Face

30th July 1973

The crazy woman chanting like a monkey and pulling hippo and leopard faces demanded his attention. His tiny body roared in huge ripples of laughter. The toddler pointed at the wallpaper. The silver lady followed his gaze to a cheerful elephant ridden by a singing leopard.

"Martin, watch them dance." She said.

He rested his face on an upturned hand. The elephant marched whilst the leopard pranced along the beast's back. He delivered a carnivorous smile and sang.

"Step aboard my elephant express,

Dance, smile, whilst I smoothly progress,

Tigers, lions, they don't bother me,

My partner here will swat 'em with a tree."

The animated pair burst into hysteria. Their audience responded with hypnotic applause.

"My name is Cyril, my friend here's Bert,

Stick with us, you'll never get hurt,

We laugh and smile, we make our way

That's simply how we spend our day,

Don't you fret, we've got our friends,

And guess what? They're at the bend."

The lady jabbed her finger to another segment of the wall. A jive monkey dragged a woolly green rhino towards Cyril and Bert.

"Well howdy there, Raphael and Mike,
We're off now for quite the hike.
O.K. Bert, chimp's ready to ride,
Mike and me don't fear no pride."

The four animals pressed on with their surreal safari.
Martin's eyes glistened when the lady closed the strange show.
"That's quite enough now, Marty. Let's get you to bed."
The boy's eyes widened in defiance. The lady rested her hand upon his brow.
"What your name?" He yawned.
The lady stroked the top of his head and smoothed away the last vestiges of awareness.
"Call me, Lady Nel."
His mother cracked the door open to find her son in peaceful slumber. She sighed, certain she heard talking before returning downstairs.
"What the hell is he doing up there?"
Martin's mother shrugged at the idle figure puffing away on another cheap cigarette.
"I have no idea. I swore I heard him nattering to someone but he's soundo."
The man slouched on a liver damaged settee, puffed, took the cigarette down to the butt.
"Don't worry Rosie, he's being a typical kid."
Rose Ellis Lowe glared at her husband. Her hand tapped a bulging stomach.

"He's not just a kid, Arthur. He's our son. Soon his brother or sister will be joining him."

Arthur stood and drew his wife close.

"Sorry love, I'm still getting used to all this 'Daddy' stuff."

Rose stared into his eyes to pierce his armour of paternity.

"You ain't sorry, are you?"

Her husband dabbed the corners of her eyes, threatening a cataract of regret.

"Darling, I've never been happier in all my life. I'm just being a prat."

Rose kissed her husband. He reciprocated with a nicotine infected thrust of his tongue.

"I wish Mum was here to see this, Arthur. She'd be so proud. It aint right what happened."

Arthur drew his wife close, patting the unborn child beneath a lily patterned blouse.

"Life's cruel, love. Still, Martin is going to have a little brother any time now."

"He might have a sister. Don't you start getting fussy," Rose said.

"Don't worry Rosie, girl or boy is fine by me. I'm sure your Mum's up there somewhere looking out for you."

Lady Nel's smoky eyes smouldered from the top of the stairs. Blessed with the awareness of Martin's soon to be brother.

She brushed an ethereal hand across her brow. Brothers clashed in their early years. An invisible tear fell and dissipated upon contact with the orange furze decorating the hallway.

"I wish I could hold you, son."

She returned to the side of her grandson. She stroked the side of his head and he wriggled in a deep joyful slumber of leopards, monkeys and one kind lady.

Chapter 2 The Dance

"It's been shit hot today, love."

"Arthur, you've got to stop swearing. I heard Martin say the 'F' word the other day," glowered Rose.

Her husband shook his head. He adored being a father yet found watching his words a chore.

"I'll be more careful."

Rose rewarded her husband with a kiss.

"I don't mean to moan but Martin's sharp."

"I know, he's going to be a bleeding genius, ain't he?"

They both giggled.

"I'm going to put some music on. I've been impressed with my new deck."

"It better not be Slade. The kids are asleep after all."

Arthur raised his hands in surrender.

"You sure? I know you love it really." He teased.

"Arthur, I'm warning you."

"What about Elvis? You can't go wrong with the king."

Rose nodded. She remembered the day she heard Elvis sing Jailhouse Rock for the first time, the same day she met Arthur.

"All right, put that Suspicious Minds one on."

Arthur scuttled off to his vinyl collection.

"I'll go and check on the boys whilst you're playing around."

Martin's mother scaled the stairs. She opened the children's bedroom. She stared in disbelief at the sight of her dead mother sitting at the foot of Martin's bed. She tried to speak. No words came. A silent trail of tears eroded her left cheek. The grey haired lady reached for Martin. His small hand nestled within her own misty fingers.

"Thanks, Lady Nel. Are you going to tell me about Humpty Dumpty again?"

"Martin, it's late. Your mum wouldn't be happy if you were up all night, would she?"

Her grandson curled his lip in disappointment.

"Please? Just once more?" He pleaded.

Daniel mumbled in repose on the far side of the room.

"Shh, off to sleep with you." Ordered his grandmother.

Martin's eyes succumbed to the weight of another day in his young life.

Rose stood unable to move or speak whilst her long-dead mother played with her son.

"Mum." Her words faint, almost imperceptible with the rumbling echoes of Elvis growing ever louder.

The misty woman turned to her daughter. Seven years passed since Eleanor had slipped through the celestial veil.

Eleanor Collins stared into her daughter's eyes and did not see a mother in her mid-twenties struggling to bring up two tiny children. Before her stood a young girl whom she reared with all her love and a child eager for her mother's wisdom.

"My little Rose-a-lee." Beamed Eleanor.

Eleanor's fragile form shimmered when moon rays whispered through the window and danced with her wispy aura.

"I'm so proud of you."

"How? Oh Mum." Rose's voice failed when a mixture of anguish and joy bubbled in the pit of her throat.

Lady Nel's eyes settled on her sleeping grandson.

"He's a special one. He sees me every night and other things too."

Rose struggled to hear her mother's words. Arthur turned the King up another notch.

"Just like you, my child, he has the sight."

Rose blanched. She recalled those nascent days of the others making their presence known. However, the onset of adulthood, love and pressures of life had long subdued her talent.

Martin's mother eyed her sleeping baby.

"What about Danny? Does he see you?"

Eleanor shook her head.

"That one's more like his father."

The volume below ascended another level.

Rose glared at the door.

"I'm going to have to go now, Mum. Mum? Where are you Mum?" asked Rose.

She glanced to the ever-diminishing diamond glow. The room filled with a lavender aroma whilst Rose wiped a solitary tear from her eye. She paused for a moment in the space her mother frequented moments before and her crown tingled with a sense of pure love.

"Don't touch them, Mum, Dad, please stop it."

Rose flinched at her son's unexpected words.

"Martin? What's the matter?"

Her child said nothing more. He twisted in dreamland whilst sleep tightened its embrace.

"You all right up there?" Yelled her husband.

Rose wondered how her children slept in such bedlam. She wondered if even the end of the world would awaken them.

"I'm just on my way." Said Rose.

She guessed her husband found the beers.

"Darling, come here for a dance."

Rose sighed with elation and despair. She prayed she wouldn't wait another ten years before her mother reappeared.

She entered the living room to find her husband shirtless and without trousers. He maintained the tiniest tincture of decorum in retaining his black and yellow striped pants along with a pair of banana coloured socks. His left hand wielded a half empty glass of frothy lager and his right brandished a dying cigarette.

"Just one dance, then upstairs. What do you say?"

Rose shook her head. Her husband's once flat stomach bounced out of time with the music. His biceps begun a one way journey to the decay of complacent flab. The swelling between his legs did little to enliven her undernourished libido.

"Not tonight Arth, besides Martin might wake up. I wouldn't want him coming in on us."

Arthur sneered, looked at the floor. He discharged a coil of ash into the carpet.

"Come on Rose, one quick dance and a tumble upstairs. Besides, how do you suppose old Marty boy got here."

He grabbed his wife in a merry embrace.

"All right, just the one then." She said.

She tried to match the dipsomaniac whilst they rocked to Elvis. The stereo faded into silence. Arthur fumbled with his wife's blouse.

"Wait until we're upstairs, at least." Pleaded his wife whilst unstable hands released her breasts. Arthur's hands plunged down towards the buttons hiding the final treasure.

"Arthur." She commanded.

He shrank away. She walked to the stereo and put the King in his bed.

"It's all right; I know when I'm not wanted."

Rose shook her head.

"Arthur, I love you, but I'm not going to have Martin walking in on us now, am I? Let's go upstairs."

Rose beckoned him to follow when her foot landed on the first stair.

Her tipsy husband pretended he wasn't interested yet the growing intensity between his legs betrayed his intent.

"I'm not in the mood."

Rose's blouse fell from her shoulders. She giggled when Arthur stumbled into a scorpion sprint after her to the bedroom.

Chapter 3 Straggled Ends

30th July 1977

"Martin, I won't tell you again," roared his mother.

She glared at her watch for the thirtieth time in ten minutes, still her husband had not showed.

"What have I done, Mum?" asked her son.

Rose's eyes narrowed. She sought grains of untruth and pointed her index finger at the nib of his nose.

"Like you don't know. I know full well you've been tormenting Danny boy with those fuzzy shrinky dink things you've been playing with."

Martin stared back open-mouthed.

"But Mum, honest, I haven't."

"Don't you but Mum me, you little git. Go and play with something else or you'll feel the back of my hand."

Martin remembered the many lessons his Mum dished out regarding playing around. He'd have to play with that boring Tonka truck again. He remembered the memento on his sore backside from yesterday morning.

Rose glared at the unwanted sausages, baked beans and mash on a solitary plate.

"If that bastard comes back pissed again tonight, I'll kill him," she cursed.

Hasty hands grabbed a jubilee cup and scrubbed it dry.

"Mummy, can I have some juice?" pleaded her youngest son.

She turned on her hips ready to explode yet dragged out a smile.

"Course you can darling. A bit of orange all right for you?"

Daniel looked away, disappointed.

"I want Ribena."

Rose slammed down a glass.

"You can't have bloody Ribena. It's orange or nothing," she thundered.

Daniel backed away. It wasn't the first time he'd seen her raging of late.

"I'm sorry son. It's not your fault but we haven't got any Ribena. Do you know how much that costs?"

Daniel shook his head. His mother poured a glass of orange squash whilst the front door sneaked open.

Rose stormed the corridor to discover her husband skulking on the stairs.

"Oi, you lazy git. What time do you call this?"

Arthur dared to glance at his wrist. He tried to concentrate, yet failed to stop a sentence of slurred words.

"Half past eight. Sorry love, I didn't think."

"You never fucking think. That's your trouble. Get in here and have your bloody dinner."

Martin crept to the balustrade. He'd never seen his mother so angry.

"Rosie, I ain't hungry love. I'm tired, I feel like I'm going to throw up."

It was too much for his wife.

"Tired? Why you lazy bastard." she raged. She grabbed his arm and frogmarched him to the kitchen.

"What have you done all day except piss our money up the wall whilst our kids go without? Well?"

"Darling, there's no need for this."

"Don't you darling me. Have you any idea how hard it is to bring up two kids when their waste of a father ain't around?"

Arthur opened his arms in apology.

"We'll work something out."

"Shut it. Martin and Danny have been at each other's throats all day but you wouldn't know about that would you?"

Martin edged closer. His father cowered whilst several dark diminutive humanoid forms danced near his kneecaps. His mother and father oblivious of their presence. One brazen creature clambered onto the back of Arthur's chair.

"I'm sorry, love. It's just things have been a bit mental lately."

The shadow leapt onto Arthur's shoulders.

"Sorry ain't good enough. I need more than that. Much more."

The shadow creature clasped savage hands around its victim's throat. Martin struggled to stifle a cry.

She shoved a full plate under Arthur's nose.

"It aint even warm."

"Eat your dinner. If you think I'm throwing away good food for you, you're off your head."

Arthur brought a forkful of cold beans to his mouth, another creature gnawed upon his ankle. Martin sobbed in silence. One of the blackened wraiths turned its gaze towards their unwelcome spectator. The beast's scarlet eyes blazed in indignant resonance when they met Martin's stare. A shapeless cavity opened where the imp's mouth should have been. Martin shied away from the shadow's laughter.

Martin tried to take his attention away from his parent's war. His father disputed Rose's accusations. The ever-growing discord fed the shadow beasts a vicious vortex of dark energy.

"Get to bed, little boy," hissed the creature.

The shadow forms all turned towards Martin. They added their own threatening gestures to the child staring at the impending darkness.

He wanted to escape to his room yet stood hypnotised by the dread spectacle before him.

"Go on, fuck off!" spat a voice next to his left ear.

Martin remained rooted. Two shades broke off the attack on his father and ascended the stairs.

"Help me, help them," he prayed.

The beasts advanced. Martin melted inside. Their presence stabbed his soul. He lowered his eyes.

"Little bastard, interrupt our meal will you?"

They were almost upon him. His parents remained locked away from him whilst the nearest creature reached with a bilious claw. It almost touched his nose when a blur of white flicked it away.

"Off with you," commanded Lady Nel.

The shades shied away from her touch and congregated in the kitchen.

"Go away, hag. You can't stop us," cursed a shadow.

Lady Nel sighed. The cancer in Arthur and Rose's marriage grew stronger every day. The dark magic grew powerful in its march to victory.

"Come on Marty, go to your room."

Martin remained locked in his stance. Her chilled hand touched his brow. The foul spell the shadows cast upon him dissipated. He sprinted to his room with his grandmother in pursuit. She thanked the stars Daniel remained unaware of the drama downstairs whilst he tried to destroy his brother's Tonka truck. Martin didn't care, his six-year old mind struggled to understand the brutal belligerence from downstairs.

His grandmother tried to reassure him. Martin cowered under his sheets.

"I'm so sorry you had to see that, Marty."

Her grandson whimpered.

"Who are they? Why are they eating Daddy?"

Lady Nel struggled to find the words for a child. A few children knew of certain dark things but seldom encountered the spite Martin endured.

"I won't lie to you. They're called shadow elementals. They're eating your daddy because he and your mother don't love each other any more."

Martin's hands covered his ears.

"I'm not listening."

She yearned to hug her grandson. Alas, the curse of premature death prevented this natural right.

"Marty, you've got to be strong. Those elementals won't stop until they've done their worst. They want to split up your mummy and daddy. They'll win because your daddy is weak."

Martin's heart blazed with rage.

"He isn't weak. He can fight them, I know he can, Lady Nel."

Eleanor admired Martin's defiance.

"It's the drink. It makes him weak inside and it feeds them."

He bowed his head. He had seen the darkening around the edges of his father's essence compared to his mother's. Rose's energy flamed white and purple whilst his dad's dwindled to distant grey.

"I'll ask him to stop, Lady Nel. I'll ask him to stop drinking," pleaded Martin.

Eleanor shook her head.

"You think your mother hasn't tried? Drink is an evil thing. It saps your daddy's life force, makes him vulnerable."

She pointed to the arguing couple downstairs. The screams of his mother and father assured Martin the shadow elementals victory moved another stage closer.

"There must be something we can do. We can't just let them win."

Her smoky fingers brushed Martin's hair.

"Believe in love. Believe in your Mum and pray for your dad. Don't you fear those shadows. They can never, ever touch a child. Never, so don't be afraid of them."

Eleanor heartened when Martin took strength from her words. She feared Martin's inevitable separation from her one day. She remembered the words of her guide who told her once Martin reached eight it would be very hard for her to stay in contact.

"Lady Nel, did you ever see them when you were here before?"

"When I was alive, you mean?"

Martin nodded.

"Yes, what sort of creatures were they then?"

Eleanor wished she had the ability to clap. She managed a gentle, almost silent swishing sound.

"The same as what you see now. They don't change Martin. They don't get old, they don't tire and they always come to the same old places."

Eleanor sat at the edge of Martin's bed. She beckoned for him to sit beside her.

"When there's going to be trouble you'll always find them nearby."

Martin touched the point of his chin in deep thought. Eleanor thought he looked much older than his young years.

"You know you said there are shadow elementals, Nan?"

Eleanor's phantom heart soared when Martin called her Nan.

"Yes, darling."

"What about bright ones then? Can't they come and chase the bad ones away?"

Eleanor wished her grandson's desires could come to pass. Life, and death, would be so much easier.

"They could Marty, but they have to be invited. They can't come unless they've been asked."

Martin closed his eyes.

"Please, Mr Nice, come and chase the bad ones away."

Eleanor blew a light gust onto his face. His eyes snapped open.

"Did they listen Nan? Will they come?"

Eleanor shook her head.

"They listened, Martin, I know that, but they won't come for you. It has to be your father; he has to do it as it's him where the trouble lies. He invited the shadows into your family's life."

He thumped the sides of his legs in frustration.

"He never asked them. He never would."

Lady Nel placed her fingers to her lips.

"Careful child. You've got to keep that temper of yours under control. Do you hear?"

Martin's eyes released a torrent of tears.

"But he never asked them, Nan."

"Oh but he did. He invited them as soon as he started drinking and turned his back on your mother."

Eleanor regretted her uncomfortable words. Martin's eyes grew ever redder. She laid her spectral hands atop of Martin's to assuage his fears.

"It isn't just shadow elementals out there. There are good spirits too, very good spirits."

His cheeks dampened ever more with the never-ending cascade of misery.

"Where? I've only ever seen you and those monsters."

Eleanor indicated to the right corner of his bedroom. Martin witnessed a gentle shimmer pour into next to his toy box.

"I've looked to protect you from the darkness out there. I've tried to keep you to myself for your first few years to make you ready."

A phosphorescent form contracted and condensed. Martin thought the new guest looked like a floating baby.

"It's too late for that now Nel, my dear," said the cherub.

"Martin, I'd like you to meet someone."

Martin's voice failed and the tiny angel sat on the floor in front of the bewildered child.

"I thought you'd have at least warned him, Nel."

Eleanor tried to protest yet the visitor brushed her indignation aside.

"Have you ever seen a cloud, young man?"

Martin thought the question stupid.

"Of course I have. Everyone's seen one."

The cherub nodded.

"Well, from now on every time you see a cloud you'll think of me."

The cherub answered before Martin's question came.

"You see my name is Claude. Claude does sound a lot like cloud doesn't it?"

"I suppose so."

"I know so," said the angel.

For the first time since his father came home Martin laughed.

"That's it. That's the way."

Martin giggled as he wondered what the creature referred to.

"Laughter, it's food of the soul. It makes those horrible feelings go away."

Claude roared in hysterics and Nel joined in with his merriment. They danced across the room and Martin laughed harder than he had ever done in his young life. His spirit filled with the most wondrous feeling. His cheeks received another burst of tears, this time of joy.

"That's much better isn't it?"

Martin nodded.

"You see, I've been watching you for a while now and you know what?"

Martin waited for Claude to continue.

"You're supposed to say what, Martin."

"What, Claude?"

"Your Nanny wouldn't let me. A proper old scaredy cat she is."

"Oi, you watch what you're saying."

Claude ignored her.

"Do you think I'm scary? Sounds like that Cliff Stewart record don't it? You know the one your Dad keeps playing."

Martin's lips parted in cheer.

"It's Rod Stewart, silly, not Cliff Richard," bleated an amused grandson.

Claude held up his arms in apology.

"Ah, well it's a long way to travel and sometimes our newspapers get a bit mixed up. I'll have to have a chat with the editor of the Heavenly Messenger."

Martin wondered what they listened to in heaven.

"I suppose you think we all listen to harps up there don't you? Ah, you don't want to listen to those silly tales. It's rock and roll and lots of late nights. Not that you'd understand at such a young age, but of course you're not really that young because you've been re-incarnated for the twelfth time to to the power of forty."

"Claude, for goodness sake, remember he's only a child."

The cherub slapped his head in embarrassment.

"Oh heavens above, listen young man, will you do something for me?"

Martin agreed.

"The next time I start going on and on, tell me to shut up. Can you do that?"

"Course, but what if someone heard? They can't see you."

Claude nodded, approving of his pupils understanding.

"Very good Martin, very good, they can't hear me either you'll be pleased to know. It would be a most ludicrous situation if you were to suddenly start bellowing at the top of your voice in a busy place wouldn't it?"

The child agreed.

"The beauty is, Martin, that no matter how hard you shout at me, I can make it so nobody else manages to hear."

"How?"

Claude displayed a full set of happy teeth.

"There's no need for you to worry about all that. You just tell me what's what and we'll be fine."

Lady Nel tapped Claude on his shoulder.

"Claude, you're telling him far too much."

Martin's head swam with new knowledge. His child mind released one burning question.

"Claude, maybe you can make the shadow elementals go away?"

Claude's demeanour darkened for the first time since he visited Martin's room.

Claude shook his head.

"I can do many things. If it were Lady Nel in trouble when she was alive I might have been able to sort something out. But there's nothing I can do to make them go away."

Martin's eyes filled with disappointment.

"You see the big problem, and it is a major one, is that I'm not ascribed to you."

Claude sighed when Nel's grandson stared blankly back.

"Let me put it another way. Someone else is supposed to help you out."

"Someone else? Who?"

Claude brought his hands together.

"Someone like me. The trouble is that your helper is a bit on the lazy side and kind of lets his charges take care of their own problems."

Eleanor fussed around her grandson. He'd learnt a lot, and seen things he wasn't prepared for.

"I think you've had enough now, Marty," she said.

"But what about my helper? I want him to make the monsters go away. I want him to make Mummy and Daddy happy again."

Claude leapt onto the bed and sat by Martin's side.

"Look young Master Lowe, I can't help you. I only wanted you to know you're not alone in your fight against those creatures. Everything that happens gets written down and one day your own helper will live up to his name."

"You say you can't help me, but tell me I'm not by myself. I don't understand."

Martin dabbed at his eyes once again.

"Now, now, don't cry. I wouldn't expect you to get all of this in one lesson. Let's keep it simple and say the good souls are looking out for you because you have a rare gift."

"I think that's more than enough, Claude," ordered Eleanor.

Claude nodded.

"All right Nel, I'll just finish up. Now, as I was saying Martin, you're very special in that you can see me, you can see your grandmother and you can see those twisted shades downstairs."

Martin shuddered.

"There's no need to fear it. It'll be the making of you one day and I know when you get older, you're going to be very talented."

"It's time we were going now, Claude."

The noises downstairs ceased. The shadow elementals feasted enough for one night. Eleanor sensed her daughter's presence heading to her son's room.

"Alas, you're right my dear Nel. Well, Martin we have to go."

Claude raised himself to his full height of two feet and held out his hand. Martin accepted the divine handshake.

"It's been a proper pleasure to meet you. I do hope we'll meet again."

Martin accepted the cherub's bright energy. His downcast feelings evaporated and the two visitors diminished.

"Goodbye, Mr. Claude."

His bedroom door eased open. His ethereal guests departed. He never saw Claude again.

Chapter 4 Merry Christmas

He wondered what pub his dad was living in tonight. He didn't care in truth though. His father lost his love when he slapped his mother across the face with the back of his belt in a pique of drunken rebellion.

Martin's mother moved on since his dad left. She even regained the lost art of smiling and it wasn't unknown for her to offer a cuddle to him and his brother.

Danny was a pain. It was always 'I want this Mum,' or 'Marty won't let me play Scalextric.' His new favourite of 'it's not fair' often resulted in a slap across the head.

"Boys, get up. Uncle Dave and Aunt Julie will be here soon, then you can open your presents."

Martin's spirits lifted. He loved Christmas. His mother went out of her way to make the festive period super special.

The last one didn't go so well. Danny kept whining about a skateboard. He threw a huge tantrum when Santa didn't deliver. His father delivered a spinning right hander and gave Danny a shiner for a present.

His mother erupted. Another huge row followed and the shadow elementals partied. They sneered and joked at the blonde son who watched. Martin remembered going to his room and seeing his dead grandmother in tears.

"Shut up. It's bad enough I've got to listen to Mum and Dad without you as well?"

Martin meant every venomous word yet the anger wasn't reserved for Lady Nel. She dissipated before his eyes. He hadn't seen her since.

"You up yet?" yelled his mother from the bowels of the house.

"Yes Mum," replied Martin. He looked to his brother who showed a glimmer of life.

"Danny, let's see what we've got."

Danny answered with a pillowed grumble.

Martin threw on his number seven England shirt on followed by a pair of weary jeans. He didn't complain when his mother bought them but his favourite player was Brooking. He thrust his feet deep within the folds of his trainers and dashed to the kitchen.

At least the shadow elementals weren't waiting to ambush him. When his father left the house for the last time they followed. Martin found it was another reason not to see his father any more.

"Merry Christmas, Martin," beamed his mother. She scooped him into her arms and kissed him hard.

"Mum," he complained.

She tweaked the side of his left cheek.

"Come on son, you can't complain about a kiss from your mum on Christmas can you?"

Martin reddened and succumbed to his mother's giggling.

"That's better, what'd you want for breakfast?"

Martin cast his eyes to the living room.

"Can't we open the prezzies, Mum? Can't we skip breakfast 'cause I bet we've got a huge meal later."

Rose shook her head.

"No. You need to get something inside you, and anyway, your brother isn't here yet."

"Danny, come on." yelled Martin.

"Oi, that's my earholes you're shouting into. It won't make any difference."

"Why?"

Rose folded her arms and peered over the top of her new glasses.

"Because nobody is opening anything until Uncle Dave and Aunt Julie get here."

Martin's joy disintegrated. They didn't believe in arriving before time.

"They won't be here for ages."

Rose ignored him. She burst into rapture when a new visitor entered her kitchen.

"Danny, Merry Christmas love."

His brother leapt into his mother's warm embrace and she kissed him over and over.

"Why can't you be like that, Misery-guts?"

Martin shook his head. He'd soon be ten.

"Can I have some Frosties, Mum?" he asked.

"Course you can, darling. How about you, Danny?"

Danny agreed and with a few greedy gulps and breakfast soon nestled in their stomachs.

"Mum, can we open our presents?" asked Danny.

His mother sighed.

"We're not supposed to be opening anything until Uncle Dave and Aunt Julie get here."

Danny's bottom lip dropped and Martin put on his most miserable face.

"Oh, all right. One present each, I will pick them."

Both boys bolted for the plastic tree in the living room. Underneath lay an array of boxes. The brothers wondered whose present had the laughing reindeer paper.

"Is that one mine, Mum?" bleated Danny who pointed at the giant carton.

"That can wait. Here you are."

She handed a book sized parcel over to Danny.

"Whose it from?" asked Rose.

"It's from Uncle Jim."

Eager hands tore at the flimsy paper shield. His eyes shone with joy when he saw the picture of a footballer volleying a shot towards goal.

"Martin, look, I've got a Kenny Dalglish book."

His brother brokered a jealous grin before tearing the paper off his own present. He stared at the picture of a horse discarding unwanted junk off its back.

"What have you got, son?"

"Buckaroo," grumbled Martin thinking his Uncle had got presents mixed up.

"That's good, ain't it?"

"Terrific, Mum."

He presented his most sincere voice, yet his mother detected disappointment.

"Don't worry boys, we'll soon open up the others," enthused his mother. Danny's face lit up when he turned to page five.

Rose gestured at the black bag in the corner of the room.

"Right, tidy up the paper and I'll make you a drink. Deal?"

The brothers got up and looked forward to killing a glass of Tizer.

"I wonder who's got the big present, Danny?"

Martin rustled open the bag and chucked the paper. In a couple of months, his plastic horse would be going the same way.

"I dunno."

"I'm going to have a look. Keep your eyes peeled for Mum."

Danny shuffled around on his toes.

"But Father Christmas won't give us our presents."

Martin laughed.

"Don't tell me you still believe in Santa? That's funny."

Danny's face glowered at his brother's teasing.

"Why? He put the presents out last night."

Martin grasped the fancy label on the present.

"Mummy puts the presents out, dummy."

"She told me it was Father Christmas. If boys are naughty, they don't get their presents."

"Father Christmas doesn't exist. I thought you would have worked that out by now."

'Dear Martin. Merry Christmas and a Happy New Year. Lots of love from Dad x.'

Martin shivered, a jellyfish sting of rage punctured his Christmas cheer.

"He does exist. Mummy said so."

Martin wanted to throw the present into the bin but nudged the gift back to its home.

Danny rubbed his eyes, tears streamed down his face.

"Shut up, cry baby," he said.

He threw himself onto the settee. His mother returned with two full glasses.

"What's the matter?" she asked. Danny snatched his drink.

"He says there's no Father Christmas. He was looking at the presents."

"Grass."

He didn't say anything else. The flat of his mother's hand whacked him across the back of his head.

"What have I told you about winding up your brother?"

Martin said nothing. His tears meandered down bright cheeks.

"Well?"

"Mum, I was only trying to get him to grow up."

Another slap across the head enforced his mother's lesson.

"Don't wind him up and leave the presents alone until I say so or you'll get sod all."

Martin nodded.

"Danny, don't take any notice. I saw Father Christmas myself this morning and I made him a cup of tea."

"Did he deliver all the presents Mummy?"

Rose planted her hands on her hips.

"Yes, although I was half tempted to send some of them back," she replied as she glowered at a penitent Martin.

Both boys sipped from their glasses. The sound of a festive tune crackled back from the doorway.

"Right boys, best behaviour and don't make a mess."

The door snapped open as Rose welcomed her brother and sister-in-law.

"That's good ain't it, Dave?' gushed Julie whilst she pointed at the doorbell.

"Yeah well nifty that, Rosie. Where'd you get it from?"

Dave glanced closer at the Melodymaster box of tricks.

"East Lane market for a couple of quid."

"It does Jingle Bells, sis?"

"Yeah and loads of others of course. Wouldn't be no good to have that on at Easter would it?"

The adults laughed.

"You'll have to get me one, Dave," urged a jealous Julie.

Her husband flicked open a packet of B&H.

"We'll see if there's anything in the sale. Probably be half price then."

Rose ushered her guests inside.

"What do you want Dave? Beer?"

"It's too early for that, a cuppa'll do me fine love."

Rose hawked over to Julie.

"Cup of tea Julie? Or something stronger?"

"Definitely something stronger, Rose. Especially after the fucking day I've had."

"Mind your language, love. The kids are in the front room," admonished her husband.

Martin and Danny emerged and hurled themselves at their Aunt Julie. She rewarded each of them with a sticky red kiss.

"Easy boys, let me get my order in first," she laughed before adding, "G and T for me, Rose."

The brothers frogmarched their aunt to the front room with a reluctant Uncle Dave in tow.

"Mum, can we open the presents now?" begged an impatient Danny.

Julie fell into the settee. Her husband deposited himself into his soon to be ex-brother in law's armchair.

"Hold on lads. Let your mother get us a drink first and 'sides we've got all day yet," ordered their aunt with her strange orange hair. Her hairstylist failed in her pursuit of strawberry blonde.

"So you looking after your mum then, lads?' asked their uncle who drew in a long drag before poisoning the room.

Martin hated smoking. His mother puffed away on the dreaded sticks and he loathed the stink.

"Yes, we helped her get things ready for Christmas Day last night," said Martin.

Their uncle nodded.

"Good boys, ah, here she comes."

Dave accepted a welcome cup of tea. He gulped a mouthful and induced a tincture of pain.

"That's hot, woman."

"What'd you expect?" protested Rose whilst she delivered alcohol to her sister-in-law.

"Cheers me dears," laughed Julie who took a heavy swig from her glass.

"Now, Mummy?" begged Danny.

Rose folded her arms yet yielded to laughter.

"Oh go on then, get your brother to help you."

Danny lay knee-deep in presents before his brother even moved.

"Mum, who is this one for? Martin, what's that say? Uncle Dave, is this from you?" were just a few of his unending questions.

Martin took his time and added to his own growing pile of presents. The whole family helped distribute the gifts and at last the grand opening began.

"I didn't think you could get so many presents under that tree Rose. How'd you do it?"

"By ramming them in as hard as I could, and Father Christmas helped me out."

She winked at Danny who eviscerated the box of his Scalextric set. Martin beamed when he opened up his box of Gazelle trainers.

"Thanks Uncle Dave and Aunt Julie," he said. He ran over to kiss his aunt, causing her to blush.

"It's all right, these should help you when you're running all over the place."

He ripped open his next present. A highwayman stared back and he raced to the record deck.

"Thanks Mum, this is brill. Can I put it on?"

She laughed.

"Later on, after dinner maybe."

His heart raced with joy and entertained no disappointment. His array of gifts of comprised of an England Shirt, Millwall top, cricket bat, World Cup album, trump cards, more singles, a pair of headphones and a giant blue sports bag. He turned his eye to the one present which remained unopened.

"Well, go on open it."

Martin looked away from the sure to be expensive present.

"Come on, hurry up," urged his uncle.

"I don't want to," he replied.

His mother frowned, taken aback by her son's peculiar reluctance.

"Why not Martin? Go on, open it."

"It's from Dad. I don't want anything to do with him."

His face flushed in indignation.

"Oh Martin, don't let the bit of nonsense with me and your dad spoil your Christmas. Things are a lot nicer now and your dad's better than he used to be."

The memory of his father lashing out at him, his brother and his mother left a stinging taint on his young mind.

"I don't want it."

Rose hugged her son before sitting beside him.

"I know he hurt you, he hurt all of us but please, open it for me."

He ripped the parcel apart and shards of paper and ribbons showered onto the carpet. Before him stood a plain cardboard box displaying an orange skateboard with flashes of silver lightning. He wanted it for a long time. His father found room to pack away a set of arm guards, knee pads and a crash helmet.

"Well, what'd you think?" asked his uncle.

"It's great, really great."

His mother gave him a generous hug, her husband still loved his son. She hadn't given up on a possible reconciliation although every day brought the D word ever closer.

"Any chance of a refill, Rose?" asked Julie.

"Course, how about you Dave?"

Dave finished unwrapping a pair of plain green socks to add to his overgrowing wardrobe of unwanted clothes.

"Cheers Sis, can I have a Ruddles?"

Rose took Julie's glass and slapped her forehead.

"Fine Christmas this is, ain't it?"

"What'd you mean?"

"Crackers! I got loads of crackers and none of us have opened any."

Dave received the first gift. His reward consisted of a green crown, a whistle and a forgettable joke. Martin pulled his with Danny. He dumped a pink hair clip, an orange hat and the ubiquitous gag onto the carpet.

"You can put your hat on can't you?" ordered Aunt Julie.

He brandished his ridiculous reward.

"What am I supposed to do with this? I'm not a girl." He replied.

His uncle puckered his lips.

"Tell you what, with a bit of lipstick, a dress and your hair clip you might just pull it off."

The household exploded with laughter. Martin reddened at his uncle's daft idea.

"He's only teasing, here, I'll swap with you."

His mum offered a green man attached to a parachute.

"Cheers, Mum."

His stomach rumbled. Martin edged towards his mother bringing in crisps.

"Anyone fancy any?"

His brother dipped his hand into the glass bowl. His mother tapped him on the hand.

"Manners, we offer our guests first."

Julie picked up a fistful of crisps and asked for another refill. His uncle took his share. Martin hoped they'd leave some behind.

"Here we are, Son."

Rose ignored Danny and headed for Martin. He took an age and filled his hand with a harvest of Golden Wonders.

"Hurry up, I want some."

"I wants don't get."

Martin gorged upon a mix of prawn cocktail and coke. It was the best Christmas yet. He looked to the tree and almost spat out his drink when a spectre glared at him. His family remained oblivious to the dark shade who rested a claw on a glittered bauble. Martin no longer feared them yet there had been six months since the last visit: the day dad left.

The elemental plodded to the skateboard and bared its fangs. Martin kept calm and remembered the words of Lady Nel.

"They can't touch you, Martin. They might threaten you, they might be horrible but they can't hurt you in this realm. Never."

He took strength from the kind memory and dismissed the red eyed wraith who leapt onto the cardboard. The beast presented a blackened grin and gestured to the table next to his mother's chair.

"Are you all right, son?" asked Rose.

He grinned.

"Of course." he said, defying the shade.

The shadow gestured at the table and danced when the telephone rang. Rose picked up the phone, her cheeks reddened.

"Hello love. How are you? You having a good Christmas? That's good. Do you want to talk to Martin?"

He wanted to walk away, he wanted to ignore the dancing shadow but the phone inched ever closer.

"Hello Martin. Did you like your present?"

He paused, steeling himself for his reply in front of three sets of inquisitive eyes.

"Yeah, it's great. Thanks a lot Dad."

The shadow drew a finger across the throat. Martin inhaled deep. Rose took the phone and soon Danny grabbed his attention with childish babble.

"All right, son?" asked Dave.

"Yeah, course Uncle Dave. Today's been brilliant."

The shadow retreated under the tree. Martin's strength frustrated the imp's designs and waspish malice grew within the darkness. Martin stared into plastic branches and the shadow departed. Martin savoured his triumph and prayed he'd never see the creature again.

Chapter 5 Life With Mum

"Pass it. Come on son, give to Joe."

Martin ignored Joe 'banana foot' Wallace. He only played because his dad was best mates with Mr. Saunders. He dribbled and drew John Collins from 4L towards him.

"Oi, Marty give us the ball." pleaded a frustrated voice from his right.

The defender lunged. Martin tip-tapped his way past and sped towards Otis who remained on his line.

"Go on, son, go on," urged his teacher.

Martin poked the ball between Otis's chubby legs. He raised his hands and his team mates swallowed him in a huddle of joy.

"Brilliant, Marty," yelled Sammy, the class captain. Mr. Saunders applauded from the touch line.

"Ok lads, great goal but let's not get carried away. It's only one-nil."

Martin did get carried away, six more goals followed, five scored by Martin. Eddy Saunders knew talent and Martin Lowe's performance exceeded all he had seen in twenty years of teaching.

"Martin, come here son."

Martin obeyed and the teacher gave him a vigorous handshake.

"I never knew you played football. How comes you haven't played for your class before?"

The protégé gave his teacher a curious glance.

"I prefer playing rounders."

Eddy shook his head.

"Forget about rounders. How would you like to play for the school team?"

Martin blinked, sure he'd misheard

"What?"

"See Mr. Gibbons after school, I'll see he picks you."

"But Mr. Saunders, they're in the semi-finals. They won't want me in the team and it'll be time to move on soon anyway."

Mr. Saunders snorted with amusement and disappointment. Just his luck to find a fantastic talent when the big school beckoned.

"They will, trust me."

Eddy Saunders prediction bore fruit. The team relied on Martin in his brief tenure for Dicken's Wanderers. They reached the final and won three to one with Martin scoring two and setting up the other. He earned a place on their tiny hall of fame. His mother delighted with Martin's unexpected success.

"Mrs. Lowe, this boy can go very far."

"How far?"

"Dulwich Hamlet, Fisher, Millwall, Charlton, maybe even Tottenham or Arsenal. It depends on Martin's attitude."

Then primary school finished and Martin readied himself for his arrival at stress school.

"Right, no doubt you're used to playing what you so think is football. I tell you now, your physical education starts bloody well here," proclaimed a brute of a teacher called Ewan Harris. He slammed heavy hands together, ran a critical eye over his newest victims.

"Well, what have we got here then? Boy, what's your name?"

"Paul, Sir."

Mr. Harris rewarded him with a tap on the head.

"Not your bloody first name, Christian names are unimportant."

"Stevens, Sir."

Mr Harris scanned the boy's physique and shook his head.

"Not much meat on you is there?"

"No, Sir."

"We'll remedy that, you've got no fat and this one's got far too much."

Mr Harris took an instant dislike to the chubby boy in front of him.

"Name?"

"Butler, Sir."

Mr Harris shook his head.

"You been stuck in the sweetshop over summer, Butler?"

Laughter swelled from his classmates.

"No Sir. I've been reading about King Henry the Eighth, William the Conqueror and loads of other kings."

Mr. Harris interrupted Butler's bookish pride with a tap to his crown.

"Did I ask what you were reading?"

"No Sir."

"Tell me, did you read about Edward the First?"

Gary Butler's eyes widened.

"Yes sir. Edward the First was the son of Henry the Third, he helped crush Simon De Monfort at Evesham and became King soon after. Then he conquered Wales."

"I hate history. I hate pointless stories about what that creep did to Wales. I'm going to call you fatty and I'm going to torture you into a new body."

The laughter annoyed Mr. Harris's fragile hearing.

"That's enough. Boy, what's your name?"

"Lowe, Sir."

Ewan appraised the boy, impressed by a reasonable level of fitness.

"You like games, do you?"

Martin nodded.

"Sir, I love it."

Harris nodded.

"What sport do you like best?"

"Football is my favourite, Sir."

Mr. Harris turned away and headed to the playing field.

"Football it shall be and we'll have a game of ten a side. Lowe, you will be Captain of Silver Lightning. Fatty, I'll give you the honour of leading out The Raspberry Doughnuts."

Martin sorted his team into the positions he thought best.

"Chris, give me as much of the ball as you can, mate."

Mr. Harris prowled by the touchline and brought the whistle close to his mouth.

"OK, begin."

Martin received the ball straight back from kick-off, two defenders yielded before him and he glided into shooting range.

"Martin, on your left, I'm in acres," demanded Chris Anderson.

He ignored the order and aimed towards the cavernous gap in the far left corner. Martin drew his right foot back and kicked fresh air. A lucky tackle ripped the ball away from him and the opposition tore away and headed towards his goal.

"Get it back, tackle him," roared the static striker.

Silver Lightning failed to regain possession. Brian Larkins snapped a shot to steal the lead.

"God, you lot are rubbish." exploded their captain.

Chris turned on his partner, furious at the unfair tirade.

"You're the one who gave the ball away. One pass and I had a tap in."

Martin stared in shock at being criticised. He slammed the ball upon the centre spot. This time he'd score the goal of the season.

Silver Lightning soon found themselves two down, then three, then four and before half-time Martin captained a side who trailed by six.

"Mr. Lowe, maybe we should have one ball for you and another for everybody else?" suggested Mr. Harris.

"Welsh tosser," he muttered.

"What was that?" asked the teacher.

"Nothing, Sir."

Mr. Harris frowned, looked over to Martin's strike partner.

"Tell you what Mr. Anderson, I'll make you Captain of the side this half. Colin Conrad will go up front. Mr. Lowe can try midfield."

"But sir, I'm a centre forward."

"You'll play where I bloody well tell you. Maybe then you'll learn to pass and maybe even tackle now and then."

The Doughnuts kicked off. Martin stole possession. He discovered Chris sprinting away from his marker.

"All yours, Anderson," he screamed. The ball soared and fell into the striker's path. Silver Lightning pulled one back.

Mr. Harris folded his arms.

"Good goal, Mr. Anderson," he proclaimed.

Martin revelled in his role of creator and destroyer. Tackles and passes merged into a kaleidoscope of sagacious soccer. The score was six goals to four and with five minutes left Martin pinged another perfect ball towards Colin. Martin surged forward as Conrad's shot rebounded and the ball arrived at his feet. Martin let fly from twenty yards and the ball stung the top left hand corner. His team mates leapt onto their star player.

"Not bad, I suppose," growled the teacher. Mr. Harris kept his dour visage in place but inside he beamed at the prodigious talent. He glanced at his watch to see two minutes remained

"Not bad, Sir. That was thirty yards out and their goalie didn't even move."

"More like ten. Hardly Ray Clemence, is he? Best your team gets a move on I'd say."

The Doughnuts gave the ball away from kick-off and the football arrived at Martin's feet. He spotted Anderson and a pass sent him advancing upon the unfortunate goalkeeper.

"Go on Chris, stick it in."

Chris beat the goalkeeper and the far post.

"That'll do. Full time, good game everyone."

Martin followed his team mates off the field.

"Mr. Lowe, a word after you've freshened up."

Martin exhaled in shock to see the teacher offer a huge grin.

"Mum."

Rose dodged her excited son when he barged into the kitchen.

"Careful, dopey, where's the fire?"

"Mum, Mr. Harris has recommended me to play in the school team. He's asked me to be captain."

Rose embraced her delighted son.

"That's wonderful."

She poured out a cup of tea for her boy, who regretted taking a sip from the boiling chalice.

"Danny, Martin's playing in the school team, not bad eh?"

"Suppose so," murmured a distant voice from the living room as a brave space hero destroyed another starship.

"You could show some enthusiasm. You've got five minutes left on that thing."

Dissatisfaction rumbled back.

"I heard that, Danny. Any more lip and it'll be no Atari for a week."

Martin giggled when Earth's last hope succumbed to alien vengeance.

"Now look what you made me do!" exploded his brother.

"What's for dinner, Mum?" asked Martin.

"Bangers and mash. We always have sausages on Monday."

Martin hoped one day his mother would show a bit more imagination.

"Still, seeing as you done so well, I suppose I can churn out some strawberry ice cream for afters."

Danny moped into the kitchen.

"You've still got three minutes."

"No point. You made me lose my last life. I was on for a new high score."

"Shut up you big baby." protested his big brother.

"You shut up. Just 'cause you played a silly game of football doesn't mean I have to care."

Martin advanced upon his sibling.

"Why don't you make me shut up."

"Pack it in, you two. I've got better things to do than listen to you squabbling."

Martin issued a glare of an unpaid violent debt.

They sat at the table ignoring each other before their mother delivered their meals coated in grease and oil.

"You made plenty of friends at the new school then, Mart?"

Martin nodded.

"Plenty, mum. A lot of the boys in my class are pretty cool."

"You don't talk to the girls then?"

Martin kneed his brother under the table.

"Mum, he just kicked me."

Rose shook her head.

"I'd kick you for that as well. For the last time both of you behave."

"Girls don't play football. Anyone knows that," sighed Martin.

"Yes they do."

Both the boys turned to Rose.

"No they don't, that's stupid," said Martin.

"When I was young I played football with the boys at school."

The brothers burst into simultaneous laughter.

"Where do you think you get all your talent from then Smarty-pants? It ain't your father that's for sure."

Martin cried in hysterics at the thought of his mother on a football pitch.

"I suggest you stop laughing unless you want to wear your afters."

Martin hid his mirth in his drink. His mother presented three dishes filled with four solid globes of red ice. The family chiselled away and the conversation on Rose's sporting prowess ended.

"Mum, how come you never changed your name back to your old name?"

Rose sighed. She contemplated changing her name back to Collins, but never did.

"I couldn't be arsed. 'Sides, it's only a name ain't it?"

"Yeah, but Mum, what's our surnames though? Shouldn't we be Collins now?"

"Eat your afters. You've got more important things to worry about than a poxy surname. Your name's Lowe and that's the end of it."

She snarled out the last sentence, Martin heeded the warning. He didn't relish the thought of his mother's palm on his cheek.

"Right, I'm off to bingo tonight. Your Uncle Dave will be round to look after you later."

Danny wrung his hands and caught the cruel glint in his brother's eyes.

"No probs, Mum. We'll be sweet."

Martin couldn't wait until their Uncle sent them to their room to watch Minder. He relished the chance to give another lesson in respect.

Chapter 6 Having A Ball

Martin hit another great pass. John Wilkes put away his second. He headed to the creator who hugged the jubilant goal scorer.

"He ain't bad, is he, Tray?"

A girl of twelve brushed back a fake Lady Di hairstyle. She never got it to quite work.

"Yeah, that's two top goals he scored now, look he's waving at us."

Tracey Broad reciprocated the striker's salutation.

"Not him, you mug. He's a bloody ugly sod, I'm talking about Martin."

"What, Martin Lowe?" giggled Tracey, "He ain't all that, I mean look at his legs, like a frigging sparrow, ain't they?"

Stacey Wells blushed. She offered her best smile when he looked over.

"He's all right, Trace. Martin's the best player out there by a mile."

The game restarted. Martin urged another assault on Crowmead's defence.

"I don't think so, Stace. My boy's the one who keeps putting the ball in the net."

Stacey looked at her watch to see ten minutes remained. Tracey done her a huge favour to cajole her to come to watch the game. Stacey hated football but when Martin surged forward her skin erupted with goose-bumps.

"Not anymore," said Stacey when Martin powered the ball into the top corner.

Her best friend gasped when Stacey applauded and cheered.

"Ease up will you. They'll think we're nutters."

Stacey caught Martin's gaze when he inspected the commotion. Their eyes joined in a momentary union. Martin trotted over to the fan club with the striker escorting him.

"Enjoying the show, girls?" he asked Stacey.

"I'd say so," interrupted Tracey who gawked at John Wilkes.

"Glad you like it, didn't think birds were into football," declared the star striker.

"We ain't, just fit looking boys like you, stud."

Stacey blushed, she wished her friend used her brain.

"What's up darling? You've gone red," laughed John.

Stacey looked down eager to find a way out from her discomfort.

"Leave her alone, you muppet. It's 'cause she's cold, that's all."

Stacey fought for her breath uneasy under the spotlight of Martin's gaze.

"It's the middle of June and it's scorching. She's just shy." informed Tracey.

"Listen, it might be hot on the pitch but when you're doing nothing but watching, it gets a bit nippy."

Martin grew impatient. He met Stacey's stare and asked the obvious question.

"Listen, we're going down the café later to shoot some pool. I can show you how to play. Would you like to come?"

Stacey's heart thumped. She struggled for the right words.

"Yeah we'll come, Martin. That's only if Johnny's coming out to play though," said Tracey.

The striker exhaled when her gaze refused to leave the top of his thighs.

"See you at five then?" asked Martin.

"Get your lazy arses over here." yelled Martin's form teacher and manager.

"Sorry, Mr. Wright."

Martin waved farewell to Stacey.

"What's your name?"

"Stacey Wells," yelled the girl louder than she intended.

"Give us a break, Mart."

The cueist ignored his friend's protests. The black eased into the middle pocket despite him looking the other way when he played the shot.

"There's no need to take the piss."

"There is when I'm playing you. Go and set 'em up and watch a maestro at work."

Another ten pence piece fed the machine and the pleasant rattle of balls snaking towards the mouth of the table were more than enough reward for Martin.

"What time is it, Wilkey?"

Johnny slammed the triangle onto the table and struggled to remember the sequence of stripes and spots.

"Look at your watch. They probably won't even show."

"Who won't show up?" asked a feminine Peckham accent behind Johnny.

"We didn't think you was going to come."

"The name's Tracey, Tracey Broad, and don't you forget it."

Johnny nodded.

"You girls want a lesson in pool then?" asked Martin.

Stacey laughed.

"Reckon you can teach us then? I ain't ever used one of these before."

Stacey held the cue the wrong way round. Martin came to her side and corrected her.

"Tell you what, how about we have a game of mixed doubles. Me and you against Tracey and Numbnuts."

"Who you calling Numbnuts, Big Ears?"

"Temper, temper boys," ordered Tracey. "Yeah, mixed doubles sounds good to me."

Martin handed the cue to his partner who pressed close to his side.

"Get your hand on the table and pull the stick back as far as it'll go and hit them as hard as you can."

Stacey aimed at the white ball and drew her hand back.

"Aim near the top of the cue-ball, it'll make the white move quicker with tops. I mean top spin.'

"Oi, no coaching," protested Tracey.

Stacey hit the ball dead centre and the cue ball tickled the pack.

"That's all right, there ain't much on," offered Martin when Stacey handed him the cue.

"That's what you think pal," said Tracey. She slammed in a two ball plant to the bottom corner.

"Top banana or what? Go on girl." cheered her partner.

Three more balls rattled into the pockets before she left Martin tight on the top cushion with no shot.

"I ain't having this."

Martin tried to smash the orange stripe into the corner but the white vanished into the middle pocket.

"You're getting done seven balls," beamed Johnny who sank two more. He pocketed the green only for the cue ball to disappear into the left corner pocket.

"Oh hell," cursed Martin. "Listen babe, do you want me to take your shots for you?"

"Oi, no cheating," repeated Tracey.

Stacey placed the ball into the D and focused on a purple stripe at the other end of the table.

"No, not that one Stace. Go for the one over the pocket" ordered Martin.

"That one's for later. I'm going for the purple one."

Martin placed his right hand over his forehead. He prayed she'd get the ball near the pocket for the next time. He gasped when the ball screamed into the top pocket.

"Thank God for that. Here, go for the orange one."

Stacey ignored him and knocked in a long yellow. Then a sequence of four more before leaving a tough long pot.

"Don't forget, you've still got two shots," offered Martin.

Tracey glared at her partner.

"This is your fault. Why'd you go in-off?"

"How comes she's such a good player?"

Stacey knocked the ball in first time.

"Only one on the black," protested Johnny, relieved the black was safe.

"Do what? We always play two shots on the black."

Tracey added her support to her partner.

"One on the black or we stop playing."

Martin shook his head. A sensitive palm on his arm dismissed his injustice.

"It's all right Mart, they can have their one shot."

Stacey doubled the ball towards safety.

"Great stuff Stace, where'd you learn to play like that?"

Stacey laughed.

"My old man runs a snooker club. I've been playing since I was five. This game's a piece of piss compared to snooker."

Tracey tried to double the black but the ball rattled in the jaws before springing into the middle of the table.

Martin examined a tough long pot. He took aim, drew his cue back, closed his eyes, looked away and shot.

"You cheeky bastard," moaned Tracey when the black disappeared into the centre of the corner pocket.

Stacey squeezed his arm.

"That was a great shot, Mart. We make a great team don't we?"

Martin caught her meaning and offered a warm smile in reply.

"The best. Together, we're the very best."

"Hope you're getting me something nice next week."

Martin sighed. He knew there was something he'd forgotten.

"Leave it with me, babes. I'll sort something out."

"You better. It's my fourteenth next week, I want it to be special."

The magma stare she imparted left him in no doubt.

"Course it'll be special, you've got me, ain't ya?"

The joke fell flat. Stacey turned her attention to some ten year olds playing in the park.

"Yeah. Great, a boyfriend who just keeps taking me out to that poxy cafe and takes me to football matches I can't stand."

Martin shook his head.

"Stace, that's my life. I ain't exactly flush with reddies. My mum's saving to buy the 'little git' a bike."

"Why do you call your brother that? It's not nice."

"He's always grassing me up saying 'Mum, Martin hit me' or 'Mum, Martin ain't done his homework,' and then I get a slap."

Stacey reached out for his hand and gave him a gentle squeeze.

"Well don't hit him then, and get your homework done. You'll be all right then won't you?"

"Screw the homework. Mr. Francis, threatened to give me lines the other day."

"Stop swearing, Mart. I don't like it."

Martin rolled his eyes, fourteen years old and hen-pecked to death.

"Stace, you're as bad as the old woman. Give me a break."

"Well, get me something nice next week and I'll reward you," she teased.

Martin fought to control the stiffening sensation beneath his navel.

"I'll keep you to that. You'll see."

A watch, perfect and expensive. Martin guessed the bald ponce with the grey overcoat played store detective. The police reject pretended to look at the gold necklaces for the tenth time.

"Johnny, do us a favour mate. I need Beaky to take a hike."

His friend nodded.

"Leave it to me, mate. He's bound to follow me seeing as I'm black."

Johnny proved to have the answer every time.

"Sorry mate."

"Ain't your fault is it? I'll lay it on heavy, you just get busy."

Johnny placed his hand on a giant gold chain. The alluring price tag of £49.99 caught his attention. He strolled to the counter. The store detective forgot Martin whilst Johnny edged to the exit. Johnny's pace quickened whilst his white shadow grew ever closer.

Martin snuffled the watch into his inside jacket pocket. He turned to see Johnny join a queue with a bemused investigator behind. Martin breezed past and entered the street.

"There you go, love."

Johnny handed her the chain as well as five pieces of silver.

"You having a laugh?" barked a blister faced girl with a fierce Bermondsey accent.

"Look it says 50p don't it, Wendy?"

The shop assistant flamed red. She hated her name badge.

"Don't you Wendy me. You know full well it's fifty quid, not fifty pence."

"Leave this with me, Wendy. I'll take care of this."

"Cheers, Mr. Whitby," snarled the grateful sales assistant.

"Come with me, young man."

Johnny backed away.

"Why? What have I done? Who are you anyway?"

Another name badge revealed Steven Whitby, security officer.

"Follow me."

"But I ain't done anything. I was going to buy that chain for my mum."

The security guard attempted to grab the troublemaker's arm.

"What do you think you're doing?"

"Just calm down and come with me please."

Johnny shook his head.

"I ain't going with you."

Several shoppers sympathised with the accused youth.

"I ain't done anything wrong. You're just a racist pig."

Steven blushed yet controlled his fury.

"Right, get out. I'm not having any more of this."

Johnny protested when ejected to the High Street.

Johnny headed off towards Sammy's cafe. He heard a familiar voice after a few yards.

"All right mate, did he give you any grief?"

Johnny nodded.

"Of course he did. As soon as I started chatting back and said he was racist, he backed off."

"Still, what a result eh?"

Martin showed the shiny watch to his friend who whistled in approval.

"You owe me. I won't let you forget unlike Beaky back there."

The duo laughed. Martin wondered how long before they discovered the disappearance of one lady's timepiece.

"No probs mate. Tell you what Johnny, I'll set you up a hat-trick next week and I'll buy you a Big Mac. That fair?"

Johnny shook his head.

"I didn't know you was so generous," Johnny said with happy sarcasm.

"You drive a hard bargain. All right, you can have a strawberry milkshake as well."

The boys shook hands and headed to Sammy's with Johnny determined to pinch at least one frame off his friend.

"Don't make too much noise."

Martin stared back open mouthed.

"As if I would, babe."

"I mean it. Mum's round her friend's house until later and said she trusted me. Now come in."

Stacey ushered her boyfriend into the passageway before allowing his lips to meet hers.

"Yeah, I'll really enjoy myself worrying about what to drink, what to do, where to dance and so on."

"Shut up, I want this to be a great night."

Martin kissed his girlfriend again.

"It will be, I promise. Trust me, you'll never forget this birthday."

Recognition flickered in Stacey's eyes.

"Did you get me a present? You can go straight home if you haven't got your bird something nice."

Martin put his finger on his chin as if in great thought.

"I knew there was something I was supposed to do. Babe, ain't a kiss and my company enough?"

Stacey thrust her hands on her hips.

"No, it ain't. Stop teasing me."

Martin pretended to be shocked.

"Only if you'll smile for me."

"Give me the damn present," she ordered.

Martin reached into his jacket and presented his girl a small oblong box wrapped in teddy bear paper.

"Oh Mart, that pattern is so cute."

Impatient fingers slipped back the wrapping. She sighed when she caught sight of the delicate watch.

"Martin, it's beautiful. How did you afford it?"

He shrugged his shoulders.

"No expense spared for the girl I love."

For the briefest moment the innocent pair glimpsed into each other's souls. Martin dreaded saying the L word.

"What, you love me?" she asked with desire swelling in her heart.

"Yes, oh yes. Come here and I'll show you how much."

Their lips met again but with far more passion than the brief union on the doorstep.

"Oi, you two. You coming inside or you gonna suffocate each other?"

The pair laughed before Stacey placed her hand into Martin's.

"You want another can of Carling, Mart?"

It would be his fourth and new territory for the teenager.

"Yeah go on then, Johnny. Have one yourself while you're at it."

"Cheers mate."

Martin winced when an elbow barged his arm.

"Oi, that's my beer you're dishing out, Mister."

"Oh yeah, I forgot, I have to enjoy myself but be sensible," he teased.

Stacey allowed her hand to nestle on his kneecap. Martin's emotions stirred once more.

"You know I said we should all behave?"

"Yeah?"

"Well, Mum's not back for another hour. I don't know about you but I could sure use a little lie down," teased Stacey.

Her gaze focused on the region between his thighs, nature ensured Martin responded.

"I'm feeling a bit tired. Is there room for two?"

Stacey pulled her partner to his feet.

"You better not be too tired Mr. Lowe and there is room for me to reward you."

Martin placed his can down. He allowed himself to be dragged to the stairway. Johnny and Tracey ignored the pair whilst they explored the art of kissing.

"Reward? What for?"

She cupped her hands and drew his ear towards her mouth.

"For getting me my present, being my boyfriend and saying you love me."

They entered the sanctuary of Stacey's bedroom and stared, unsure of what to do next. Stacey took the lead and her blouse fell from her shoulders. She offered Martin with his first close up glance of a young girl's treasure.

"Are they your tits?"

Martin regretted uttering his ludicrous question the moment he spoke.

"Nah," she said with her best sarcastic tone, "tell you what, see if this will help you."

Stacey released the clasp of her bra. Her upper flesh lay open to inspection to her wide-eyed lover who placed nervous fingers onto her nipples.

Stacey reached out and undid the buttons on his shirt. She purred whilst her fingers explored the fine growth of new-born hair on his chest. Her fingers descended, eager to find new flesh to play with.

"Stacey, I don't know if we should go further."

She kissed him again.

"Shush, this is so right Martin."

His belt yielded. His trousers fell to his ankles. At Stacey's urging he freed his feet from shoes and socks.

Stacey's dress descended and both of them stared in wonder at each other. Stacey pushed Martin to the bed. She focused on the swelling within his briefs. She cast aside her tights and beckoned for Martin to remove the final white cotton barrier.

She allowed him to pull down her panties and revealed her most precious gift. She stood immobile as he studied her body in teenage rapture. She groaned whilst he stroked her over and over. She tucked her fingers into the elastic holding his aeroplane patterned y-fronts and pulled. The young lovers collapsed onto Stacey's bed and succumbed to naive love.

"It was beautiful, Stacey."

The pair gazed at each other's fresh bodies.

"I'll do better next time, Stace."

"Shush," she whispered. She stared at the clock.

"Damn."

"What's wrong, where's the fire?" joked Martin.

"My mum is where the fire will be if she catches us. Hurry up and get dressed."

Martin laughed when his girlfriend threw her clothes on.

"Need this, do you?" Martin teased as he twirled her bra around with his right index finger.

"Quick, help me get it on."

The bra found its proper place. They shivered when the front door sprang open.

"Downstairs, now." she ordered.

The couple kissed and Stacey went to greet her mother. Martin, stared at the back of Stacey. He vowed they would always be together no matter what.

Chapter 7 Going Shopping

"I don't bloody believe it."

Mr Pathan's shop offered a heavy set of shutters. Martin thirsted for coke and the nearest newsagent laid half a mile away. He jangled shrapnel in his pocket and set off.

He looked at the threatening clouds ready to spew rain. He quickened and waved when Tracey Broad appeared on the other side of the road.

"Wotcha Trace," he yelled.

"All right, mate. Where you off to then? Buying something nice for Stace?"

He crossed over; he didn't want all of South London to hear.

"With what? I've got no dosh until Saturday."

"Ain't stopped you before has it?" she sniggered.

"I don't know what you mean," he replied.

"Johnny's told me everything about what you get up too. Heard you had a right old thieve up the other day."

Martin shrugged.

"Well, Stace wanted that new Paul Young record didn't she? Anyway, you got the Thompson Twins didn't you?"

Tracey twisted her lips in reluctant agreement.

"Suppose so. I wanted Wham really though, that George's well nice."

"Johnny reckons he's gay."

"That's the biggest load of tosh I've heard. He's got girls chasing after him all over the place. If he was gay he'd look like Boy George wouldn't he?"

"Maybe."

"Ain't no maybe about it."

Martin sighed.

"Mart, you and Stace doing anything tomorrow?"

"What, this Saturday?"

His friend's face glowed in impatience.

"Right old Einstein you are."

"We can't do anything until five. We've got to play a match against some team from the Elephant. We could go top."

"I know. I didn't know you was as thick as Johnny. I was thinking of going to watch a film at the Coronet afterwards."

Martin relished the thought of being at the back of the cinema with Stacey.

"How we going to afford it? Four of us going is going to be pricey."

Tracey tapped the end of her nose.

"You leave it to me. My sister works there and if I do her a couple of favours, I reckon she'll sort it."

Martin said a grateful prayer to Karen Broad.

"Sounds good to me, Trace. Are you going to see Stace?"

"No, got to see Aunt Alice. I'll give her a call later. I'll give you a shout before you shoot off to your match to let you know if the film's on or not."

"Nice one, catch you later Trace."

"No probs, Mart. See you tomorrow."

He soon bought his drink and thanked the heavens he didn't get wet. He rubbed his eyes when Mr. Pathan walked across the other side of the high street. The kind old shopkeeper never left work. He shivered, shook his head and headed home.

"You all right, Mr. Pathan?"

The shop-keeper presented a toothless smile. He nodded, trudged past and didn't look back. Martin stood bewildered whilst Mr. Pathan faded into the horizon.

A shade adorned in the apparel of an umber sheepskin coat shuffled into sight from twenty yards behind Mr. Pathan. Martin shrank into the white fence on his left. The creature drew a line across its throat.

Martin looked for witnesses but remained alone.

"What do you want?" Martin asked.

The creature made no sound. Martin sensed cruel amusement gurgling from a hidden mouth. Two molten eyes burned into him and the shadow pointed its finger at Martin's chest.

Martin remembered an ancient lesson from Lady Nel; the creatures can't hurt you. He didn't walk away from the shadow but towards it, furious one should return after four long years.

"Well come on then."

The shade shied away from Martin's unexpected belligerence. The ill-dressed beast backed away.

"What's up, you a coward? Come on, let's have it."

Martin sprinted towards the shade. The shade turned and fled. Martin chased but the pace of the phantom took the elemental far away. His head throbbed and the world changed.

"Look where you're going, you lout," cursed a grey-haired harridan not pleased at almost being knocked to the ground.

Martin said nothing but stared into where the beast had been.

"Nutter, I'll call the police."

She walked away, still muttering. Martin shrugged and made his way back home.

"Martin, do us a favour and get me some fags?"

"Why can't Danny go? I've only just got in."

His mother glared at her truculent son.

"Why do you always answer me with another question? Just get my fags."

She thrust money into his left hand.

"You'll have to go down to the other newsagents though. The Indian shop is closed, poor old Mr. Pathan passed away last night."

Martin froze.

"Mum, I just saw him ten minutes ago, near the fire station."

Rose Lowe inhaled.

"You must have been mistaken, Mart. He died of a heart attack last night."

Martin nodded to keep the peace and said a silent prayer.

Chapter 8 Turn It Off

The nightmares returned. He tried to take solace with Stacey yet shades threatened him and all he owned.

"What do you want? Why don't you just leave?"

The creatures ignored his pleas, sharpened their blackened nails. He grew ever tired in his sleep from the eerie battle. The circle of hate about him intensified each passing night.

"You cannot beat us."

It was the first time they had spoken. Their honeyed voices soft yet laden with razorwire.

"Who are you?"

"We are you. You make us, not your mother, your father or your fool brother. You give us power."

Martin's dreamy paragon asked for Lady Nel.

"She cannot help you. You sent her away or have you forgotten?"

He sank to his knees. The phantoms crept closer.

"Surrender, take my hand. Join us and let the darkness flow."

Martin fought the malodorous heart of the wraith who stared into the sweaty folds of his face.

"I won't surrender."

Martin garnered strength from within. He stood and roared in a voice older than his tender years.

"Go away, I never want to see you ever again."

The creature scuttled to the edge of his vision with dark disciples close behind. Martin recognised the distorted road where he saw Mr. Pathan earlier. He heard the shopkeeper calling for his wife and children.

"Get out of here Mr. Pathan, go to the light."

"Martin, is that you? I can't see anything."

Martin shouted for him again.

"How can he find the light when there is none? We won't let him."

Martin groaned when the shapes formed a cancerous ring across the road. Mr. Pathan spun and fell amidst their number and disappeared into the labyrinth of the lost.

"Let him go. He's done nothing to you."

Martin went to cross but a number twelve bus drew in front of him.

"He called us Martin. Look for yourself."

The shadows allowed Martin a glimpse of Mr. Pathan's disturbed world. A young Asian youth of fifteen bent himself forwards over the shop counter. Mr. Pathan indulged himself in a vile display of forced affection.

"All for the sake of love." joked the shadow with the sheepskin jacket.

"Want to see more?"

The image changed. Mr. Pathan held his wife down on the bed before tying her wrists and legs to each corner. He licked the edge of a savage belt.

"Unclean bitch," he yelled.

The belt tore across her body before he inflicted a brutal display of butchery. She whimpered through a handkerchief gag.

"Love, love, love," sang the Shades in their parody of the Beatles.

"Have a look at this then, Martin."

The image changed for one last time. Mr. Pathan opened the door to his daughter's bedroom.

"She's only five." he cried.

Martin's stomach finally failed.

"Light's out for poor old Mr. Pathan, eh Mart? You won't believe the things we see."

Mr. Pathan stood alone again under the shade's taunting. He cowered on all fours, a wretched beast of a man, not the hard working hero Martin believed him to be.

Martin cursed him. Not for the brutal scenes he'd witnessed but for his spirit to awaken the shades.

"Bastard."

The shades agreed.

"Oh yes, he's one of us. As you will be one day Martin."

"I could never do that."

Laughter cawed back.

"Never say never. We know what's going to happen. It's going to happen real soon."

"Just go away."

The shades taunted him. He turned his back on them.

"Where'd you think you're going? Did we give you permission to leave?"

Martin focused on a white fence ahead of a block of Peabody flats.

"You can't shut us out. You can still help Mr. Pathan if you want. Maybe you can show him the light."

"He can go to hell. Do me a favour and go there yourself."

The shades screamed in triumph. Martin ignored them and walked away.

Chapter 9 A Welcome Break

"Martin, time to get up, it's eight o'clock."

The images of the dark elementals and Mr. Pathan still burned his mind.

"Hurry up if you want your breakfast. Danny's had his already."

"It's all right, Mum. I'm not hungry. Must have been something I ate last night."

"Nice way to talk about your mum's cooking."

Martin heard the sound of a skeleton attacking his brother in the living room. He wondered how his mother let him play video games so much.

"Cup of tea then for Mummy's little soldier," she teased.

"Yeah, wouldn't mind one please."

He grabbed the cup and sipped from the rim despite it being far too hot.

"Let it cool down, dopey. Anyway, you should have something inside of you."

"Sorry Mum, I had a really bad dream last night."

Rose ruffled his hair, placed two slices of toast in front of him.

"Eat them for me. Trust me, you'll feel better for it."

He didn't want to touch the bread but once he bit, he savoured the velvet seduction of butter.

"Want another couple?"

Rose knew her son. Two more slices appeared before the hungry teenager.

"So what's the dream about then? You can tell me you know."

Martin told her about the shades and that Mr. Pathan was very cruel. Rose always suspected something wasn't right about the bald little man.

Martin's revelation lifted his spirit. So long he'd kept these thoughts to himself.

"I used to get the same things as you when I was younger. It's your Nan's fault you know, she had the gift and passed it on."

"I don't want it, Mum. I don't want to see dead people; I don't want to see those horrible creatures."

Rose placed her arms around her son's shoulders.

"Then don't. Tell it to stop. It did for me and it will for you as well."

She dabbed a tear from Martin's cheek.

"Really? As easy as that?"

"Really," his Mum reassured.

"Oh, I forgot to tell you son. Stacey rang yesterday and said she'll be round at ten. That all right?"

Images of demons and deviant shop keepers vanished. The thought of his girlfriend elated him.

"Course it is, Mum. You know she'll be family one day."

Rose chuckled at the glint in her son's eyes. She hoped his prediction would come true. She adored Stacey and there were far worse girls he could chase.

"You never know. Anyway, hurry up and get yourself dressed. I'm not having her come round with you in your pyjamas."

"Dressing gown actually, mother."

Rose tapped her son on the head.

"Oi, don't get lippy with me young man and don't call me mother. You make me sound ancient.'

Martin retreated to the haven of the door.

"But you are."

He ducked a well-aimed but slow slipper arrowed at his head.

"Where we going then?"

He responded with a wink.

"Wait and see."

Stacey pursed her lips. She hated surprises.

"Come on tell me."

They carried on walking and entered the shopping arcade.

"Just a bit further and you'll see for yourself."

His girlfriend looked left, right and sought her reward.

"Mart, where we going? There's nothing here except shops and a train station."

The mischievous smirk on Martin's face widened.

"We're going on a train are we?"

Martin shrugged.

"Might as well, I've got a couple of tickets."

He passed her a ticket displaying Hastings.

"We're going to the seaside. Mart, I ain't been in ages."

Martin warmed at the sight of Stacey's joy. He accepted his reward of a long sensuous kiss. A wizened man huffed his disapproval.

"Bloody cheek, you ought to be ashamed at yourselves carrying on like that."

"Sod off, Grandad."

The young couple laughed at his reddening face.

"I ought to give you both a clip around the ear. Bloody no respect."

The pensioner advanced and rolled up his sleeve.

"What, you think you're hard enough? Come on then you old git."

"Why, you young punk. I'll tell the police about you. You see if I don't.'

The unwanted guest disappeared into the morning air.

"What the bloody hell did you do that for?"

"He's getting on my nerves, Stace. I ain't having him talk to you like that."

"What if he goes to the police? He didn't look too happy."

Martin's lips parted in derision.

"He ain't going to the Old Bill. I've seen his lot before, all high and mighty and then they back off when you front 'em up. I ain't having him spoil your day."

Stacey accepted Martin's hand and their train pulled into the station. The couple secured a cosy compartment to themselves.

"You ever been to Hastings before, Stace?"

Stacey leaned back deep in thought.

"I don't think I have, you know. If I did, I was only little."

"It's going to be blinding. Just you wait until I get you in the caves."

Concern travelled across Stacey's brow.

"Caves? I thought it was all amusements and stuff."

Martin released an evil laugh

"There's plenty of stuff all right, just you wait and see."

"I aint happy about caves. What'd you want to take me there for anyway?"

His tongue carved a trail across his top lip.

"It'll be quiet, dark and we won't be disturbed. I think you can work it out."

Stacey's eyes bulged in revelation at her boyfriend's designs.

"You want to shag me in some hole in the ground. Leave off.'

"No, it'll be great Stace. You know how hard it is to get any privacy. I can't do anything round my place because my brother's always in and there's always someone round your house."

Stacey shook her head.

"It'll be all mysterious. I mean there's not many who have had a tumble in some old smugglers place."

"Smugglers? Are there smugglers around then?"

Martin laughed.

"Not now silly, hundreds of years ago there was though."

"Who you calling silly?"

The train lost speed, a new platform came up on their left. Martin guessed they'd have passengers to keep them company.

"Only kidding. Think about it, it'll be perfect, won't it?"

"I can imagine my arse on some rotten bit of rock with you on top of me. Sounds more painful than special to me."

Two sets of doors opened and their precious moments of privacy ended. A man in an undersized tracksuit sat in the next row of seats.

"We'll stand up then. We ain't done it that way yet."

Their new guest pretended not to take any interest but the narrowing of his brow betrayed disapproval.

"Stace, trust me, it'll be fine."

The train pulled into Hastings at one P.M. Martin guided his girlfriend to the sea front.

"What time are we going to get a train back? I ought to let Mum know."

Martin rolled his eyes.

"Stace, we've just arrived and you're talking about going home. Tell you what, we'll get the seven thirty."

Stacey, scanned her new location.

"Can you see a phone? It's best I let her know."

Martin led her to a booth.

"All right, that's sorted. We going to get something to eat then?" asked Stacey.

"I'm starving as well. I'm hungry for you, ain't I?"

"Martin, I want to see Hastings first and I want something to bloody eat."

They found a cheap café opposite the dodgems. Stacey savoured a fatty sausage roll and a lukewarm polystyrene cup of tea whilst Martin dined on chips and coke.

"This is the life ain't it? When I'm older I'll bring you down here every year."

A few grains of rain drizzled onto Stacey's face but did not dampen the joy of Martin's promise.

"That'd be beautiful."

"You want a chip?"

Stacey grabbed an onion vinegar saturated lump of potato and let it dissolve in her mouth. She wished the chippies in South London could make theirs taste as good.

Martin glanced over to the source of tinny music and lasers being fired.

"Let's have a go in the arcade. I'll see if I can win you a cuddly toy or something."

"Do they do Winnie the Pooh?"

Martin stole his girlfriend's hand.

"I ain't got a scooby. Must have something worth having though."

They exchanged silver for copper. Martin tried the impossible mission of throwing a pair of metal pincers at a lump of fluff.

"You ain't no good, are you?"

The pink panther slipped from the steel claw once more. Martin shrugged.

"It's a fix. If you think it's so easy, you have a go."

Martin slipped in another coin. Stacey took her place at the helm. She pulsed the claw forward and aimed at the creature's left thigh.

"It'll never work."

Stacey allowed the hand to descend and cheered when it snared the panther's leg. The crane climbed and she her breath whilst the toy tumbled into the black hole of triumph.

Stacey whooped and grabbed the panther's chest.

"I thought you said it was hard."

Martin shook his head.

"You jammy git. Bet you can't do it again."

Stacey hugged her new acquisition and looked across the arcade.

"Luck's got nothing to do with it and I've got what I wanted."

She glided to the Penny Falls and handed the panther to her partner.

"What'd you reckon I should call him?"

"Buggered if I know. How about Rupert?"

She burst into fit of a giggling.

"Rupert. Rupert's a bear, you muppet. I'll call him Claude."

Martin's memory flashed back to when he first met the shades and his grandmother's guardian.

"Yeah, call him Claude. It's a good name for a puppet."

Stacey tapped Martin on his nose with her fingertip.

"He's not a puppet Martin, he's my good luck charm, our good luck charm. He'll always remind me of this day."

Stacey threw her arms around her boyfriend's shoulders and gave him a heartfelt kiss. She wished she could have stayed in the moment forever.

Chapter 10 Moving On Up

Panic. Martin double checked his bag, his room, his wardrobe, everywhere he looked yielded no discovery.

"Where are they?"

"What are you looking for?" asked his mother.

Martin rushed into his brother's bedroom.

"My boots. If I don't find them I've had it."

His frustration worsened when he found zero.

"I swear if he's hidden them I'll kill him. I ain't joking either, Mum."

He wrenched open Danny's wardrobe and hunted through his brother's Superman collection.

"Now that's enough. I'm not having you mucking up your brother's room because you can't put things away properly."

Martin glared at his mother in disbelief.

"Are you stupid? It's the Cup Final today. Mum, sometimes you're more of an idiot than that brother of mine."

Martin braced himself for his mother's furious tongue.

"You cheeky git, if it wasn't for me, you'd be with that pathetic father of yours getting a slap every night when he came home pissed. If I'm stupid what does that make you? Well?"

Martin backed away from the heat of her rage.

"Mum, look I just need those boots, I'm sorry for having a go."

"Shut it. You're pathetic and getting on my nerves. Always moaning about what Danny's done and what homework you've got to do. Well, I tell you what Martin, my fucking heart bleeds for you."

Martin withdrew to the door. His mother's snarling face and swearing unleashing a side he'd never seen.

"Yeah, sneak off to your room. I bring you both up, work stupid hours down the supermarket and all you ever do is frigging whinge. Go on, piss off and get out of my sight."

He stared at the carpet and crept into his room. He'd never seen his mum so angry. He winced at the sound of sobbing from his brother's room. He sat on his bed and examined the clock. Martin contemplated the unthinkable: throwing a sickie.

His stomach blanched at the thought but seeing his mother so upset struck deep. He vowed to do more. He hoped she'd forgive him. Martin cried real tears for the first time since his father left.

He heard the door squeeze open and a gentle hand settled on his shoulder.

"You looking for these, soldier?"

A pair of three striped football boots fell beside his feet.

"It doesn't matter, Mum. I didn't mean to be such trouble."

His voice cracked with emotion. Rose stroked her son's cheek.

"It does matter. I'm sorry I snapped at you just now, it's been a tough few days."

Martin wished his mother didn't have to work those extra two hours. She worked so hard and the bags under her eyes betrayed her sagging energy.

"Mum, if you don't want me to go to the match I'll stay and help out a bit. Me and Dan could do a lot more round the house."

Rose's heart swelled after his last sentence. She struggled to contain the surge of pride within her.

"Of course I want you to go. I want you to go out there and win because I'm so, so proud of you."

She embraced him and pointed at his boots.

"Hurry up and get dressed before the minibus gets here. Your brother, myself and your Uncle Dave and Aunt Julie will be along in your Uncle's Cortina."

Martin thanked his luck that he'd be with his team-mates. The thought of his Uncle's dodgy driving and his Aunt's incessant babbling about last night's telly and aerobics classes did little for his enthusiasm.

"Will do, and Mum?"

Rose looked back at her son from the passageway.

"What is it, son?"

"Thanks for looking after me and my brother, thanks for everything."

The anguish she released seemed an ocean away from her maturing son. She restrained the urge to cry and rewarded her son with a bear hug.

"Just play your game, you soppy sod. You better bloody win though."

"Remember what we were working on in training. Martin, I want you to boss midfield and pump those balls out to Wilko all day long. Their centre back's big but no pace. Keep it simple and give me a game to remember."

The footballers cheered when their leader put on his armband.

"No probs, Mr. Turner. Come on lads, let's get out there and win."

Martin led out the players and claimed the pitch. Hartin spotted his family along with Stacey and Tracey cheering like howler monkeys in the main stand.

"Savour it son. You could easily play non league level and well beyond if you apply yourself. You want some of this don't you?"

Mr. Turner's words fired Martin's desire. He imagined himself leading out a team in the cup final. He dreamt of winning the ball off Jimmy Case, bamboozling Terry Mcdermott and smashing the ball past Clemence before claiming the cup and accepting the acclaim of the fans.

He stood face to face with the slow centre back his teacher told him to torment.

"Heads or tails?"

"Tails never fails, ref," said Martin.

The official flicked the coin. The silver came down in Martin's favour.

"You want to change ends?"

"No, you're all right."

Martin sneered at the giant ginger-haired defender, trying to intimidate him.

"Right, congratulations to both of you for getting to the final. Before we kick off, I'd just like to get a few things straight. My word is law. If I blow my whistle you stop play until I tell you to carry on. If you give me lip, you'll be rewarded with a place in the book. If you commit a nasty foul, you'll go in the book. If you swear at me, the linesmen or get shirty, you'll go in the book. Understand?"

"Yes ref," said both of the bored captains.

The calls of impatience from the stands increased in volume. However, the referee persisted in pedantry.

"We will kick off at exactly eleven o'clock. You will refer to all of us as Sir. Do you understand?"

Martin nodded. He wanted action, not the instructions of the world's fussiest referee.

"Yes Sir," replied both captains in unison.

"Right, now that's all resolved I'd like to wish you good luck and enjoy the game."

His two officials took their positions on the wing. The referee pursed his lips, raised his left arm and blew hard on his whistle.

Martin flicked the ball back to his defence. He slipped away from his marker as the ball sprung back and forth away from the opposition. He told them to keep possession, to not let the ball go.

The midfielder tucked himself away ten yards away from the opponent's penalty box. Joey Barnabas smashed the ball high and long.

"Joe, keep your head." he screamed.

St. Andrew's took possession and attacked. Martin slid in, got the ball and aimed the ball at their striker.

"Foul, stop the play," ordered the referee after he'd blown his whistle.

Martin turned around, stunned.

"What for? I won the poxy ball, didn't I?"

The official stood in front of Martin so close he smelt the remains of a tuna dinner from the night before.

"No, you didn't. You fouled that boy and for your lip you can have one of these."

The captain was flabbergasted when he received a yellow card.

"Name?"

"What are you booking me for? I ain't done anything."

Martin's team mates milled around him. Mr. Turner held his arms out wide and bellowed at the referee from the side-lines.

"I made it perfectly clear I will not have any swearing or abuse. Also, your tackle was late, so if I wanted to I could actually send you off. Name?"

Fury swelled inside Martin. He wanted to punch the joker on the nose. He clenched his fist and a firm hand grabbed his shoulder.

"Leave it, we need you on the pitch."

A face of empathy found the wisdom hiding in Martin's head.

"All right John, I'll do my best."

The boys from St. Andrew's waited whilst the referee continued his sermon. Their captain calmed the storm and received the same reward as his opposite number.

"What you booking me for?"

"For trying to do my job. Now, I'll have your name as well as the other twit over there."

The official beckoned Martin forward.

"Best you hurry up with your name or I'll bloody well send you off."

"Martin Lowe."

"And you?"

"Freddy Young, Sir."

The referee ordered the game to continue, satisfied with his display of authority.

Martin took possession once again and spotted Johnny bend his run around the back of the left back. Martin curled an accurate pass over their centre back and into the path of a gleeful striker.

"Get in there," yelled Martin, who raced towards his team mate and best friend.

"Fantastic ball, mate. I swear you're getting better and better."

The two embraced before being swamped by their ecstatic team. The referee's whistle dismissed their moment of joy.

"Get back to the centre spot, look lively or I'll get my cards out again."

The official's face reddened whilst Martin's side trudged back to their own half.

"I don't think he's too happy with us going one up, Johnny."

"Ain't you heard, Mart? Rumour has it that he's the uncle of one of the players from St. Andrew's. He didn't muck around booking you did he?"

Martin shook his head.

"I thought that was because he was a prick."

"You're right there, mate," laughed Johnny.

The game restarted. Martin's side controlled the game. Time and time again he spearheaded their attacks. St. Andrew's defensive unit held out until the seventeenth minute. Stevie Harris connected with a header and smashed the crossbar, the ball arrived by Martin patrolling the edge of the D. He met it on the volley and the ball nestled in the top corner.

"Have some of that you pricks." yelled a triumphant Sammy Hall who leapt onto his captain. Martin glanced over to the touchline to see his coach embracing his assistant. He sighed when the chirping of the referee's whistle soared in intensity.

"Two-nil, come here young man."

"Who me, ref?" asked Sammy in bewilderment.

"I have a present for you."

The referee reached into his pocket and brandished a red card.

Martin and his team mates stared at each other in utter amazement. Their disbelief dissipated and transformed into rage.

"You can't send him off, ref. What'd he do? He ain't even had a yellow."

The maelstrom of abuse continued. The official pointed to the changing rooms.

"He screamed a swear word. I'm not having that sort of language on my pitch. Any more lip and someone else will be following him."

Martin placed a consoling hand on the defender's shoulder.

"It's not your fault. This bloke's a disgrace."

Tears dropped onto Sammy's orange shirt. Martin promised to win the match for him.

"Don't cry, we ain't losing. They're useless and even a dodgy ref ain't changing the result."

Five more bookings were issued towards Martin's team. Three more goals in St Andrews's net finished the job. The opposition replied with one token goal of consolation.

"Brilliant boys, absolutely brilliant," gushed the coach who hoisted Martin onto his shoulders.

"Mart, this is yours son."

He caught the match ball. Three goals from a midfielder in the cup final were more than even he dreamed for.

"Which reminds me, where's that ref?"

Mr. Turner spotted the official scuttling to the changing rooms with his attendants close behind.

"I want a word with you," roared the teacher.

He broke into a sprint. Mr. Turner's pursuit ended when the headmaster headed his way with a huge grin.

"Delightful performance by your boys, Mr. Turner. I have to say that you did rather well, didn't you, young man?"

The head presented his hand and an embarrassed captain received the ultimate honour.

"Thanks Mr. Spearman. It's been a great day."

"You were all a credit to the school Mr. Lowe. Still, this is your time now."

Several gentlemen in suits stood next to a table in the middle of the pitch. St. Andrew's trudged to receive their losers' medals. Martin shivered at the sight of the silver shield in the centre.

"C'mon lads, time for your reward and where's Sammy?" asked Mr. Turner.

Martin spotted the disgraced defender heading towards them. A wide smile filled his face.

"Sammy, over here. You're the real hero mate."

Martin led his team over to the defender.

"I said we'd do it for you, Sammy."

The team received their winners' medals. Martin hopped in impatience whilst the team filed away to allow him to accept the prize.

"Ah, the man of the moment."

Another hand pumped Martin's own.

"I'm Mr. Harrington, chairman of Bartley Vans. We've been sponsors for the last ten years and we hope to do so for the next ten years as well."

Martin nodded and gazed at the massive trophy.

"I can say with all sincerity it was a delight to watch your team's performance and without further ado I wish to present you with our shield."

Martin almost threw the reward over his shoulder. He raised it to the front of his forehead and absorbed the adulation from the supporters. He imagined himself holding the FA Cup aloft in front of thousands of fans.

Martin re-joined his team mates to show off their prize.

"Sorry captain, but we've a couple of other minor details we need to go over with you." said Mr. Harrington.

He handed a small box over to the young midfielder.

"That's your winner's medal. I trust you'll take good care of it?"

Martin responded with a firm nod.

"And this is for you as well. There you are, man of the match."

Martin slid his young wrist around the statuette of a footballer with a golden ball at his foot. Mr. Turner helped relieve his load along with and two team mates.

"I've been trying to get my hands on this trophy for over ten years. Thank you all for making it happen."

The teacher's eyes glistened when he took the shield.

Stacey scampered across the pitch and he handed his trophy to her.

"Mart, you were brilliant. I ain't half glad I'm going out with the best footballer and the best looking one."

He rewarded her with a deep kiss.

"Can you look after that for me? I want to be with my team for a few seconds. I'll catch up and we can go to the café for a proper celebration."

The pair kissed again. Stacey flushed with jealousy when Martin sped over to his colleagues for a lap of honour. She tucked the trophy under her arm and brandished the award in front of Tracey.

"He ain't the best looking geezer, Stace. Everyone knows it's my Johnny."

"What'd you bring us down here for then?" asked a youth dressed in a suede leather jacket with the words 'Sweet' shaved into his hair.

"Will you stop moaning? You don't think I'd rather be shagging Carol than to listen you mugs going on all day? You think I want to watch those idiots pretending to be Glenn Hoddle?"

"Charlie, we didn't have to come did we? I'm dying for a fag."

Charlie spat a globule of phlegm towards the pitch.

"Course we had to come. Harris has been right on my case and promised to drag me here himself if I didn't show."

"Geezer's a tosser, Char. Still, our midfielder wasn't bad, was he?"

"You mean to tell me you watched that pile of crap, Warren? Yeah, he's good but I bet he can't knock back five cans of Tennant's Super before he up chucks. I bet he don't smoke either and that bird he's with is a moose." growled Charlie

Murmurs of agreement filled the air.

"I bet he ain't even screwed her. I bet they're both virgins."

Fresh laughter pealed across the stands. Charlie cursed when Mr. Harris looked towards them.

"Oh cobblers, he's coming over."

"Mr. Stead, what are you lot up too?"

Charlie held his hands open in protest.

"We're cheering the team, Sir."

Charlie spat the word Sir.

"Glad to hear it, now get your arse down here and give me a hand."

The youth withdrew his size eight Dr Martens from the blue plastic seat in front of him.

"All right lads, you heard teacher. Let's give him a hand."

The four boys launched into a round of mock applause. Charlie swore the teacher's moustache quivered.

"Have you any idea how many times I had to listen to that joke, Stead? I'll tell you, bloody thousands, now get down here."

Charlie swept his palm across his forehead.

"What for?"

"Because I told you too." screamed their teacher.

"Sorry Sir, what I mean is, I have to know because of my condition."

Mr. Harris passed over the tiny barrier and towered over his rebel.

"Condition? Do tell me Mr. Stead, I can't wait to hear this."

Charlie laid the soles of his boots back across the ridge of the seat in front.

"It's my back, Sir. I can't lift nothing, if I get injured it'll be your fault."

Mr. Harris snorted and pointed to the field.

"Don't you give me any of that. Get down there and clear up now."

The teacher yelled out the last word. Charlie didn't stir.

"I ain't going, Sir. I ain't ruining my life for a bunch of muppets."

Charlie wriggled in his chair when Mr. Harris ground his fists together.

"I ought to batter you Stead, and the rest of your cronies."

Charlie wanted him to try. He relished the chance of sticking his steel toe caps into the teacher's huge nose.

The teacher walked away.

"Monday, Stead. My office, nine sharp. We'll see if you're so bold then, won't we?"

Stead looked behind him once the teacher re-joined his team.

"I've had enough of this. Who is coming for a snout?"

The quartet agreed, trudged off into the darkening afternoon.

Chapter 11 A Harsh Farewell

Martin rubbed the statuette on the mantelpiece. He half expected a genie to knock on the door and offer trials with Fisher. Nothing happened, except for the knowledge he helped his school win the shield for the first time in their history. They'd never forget him.

"Martin, phone."

He returned the trophy and struggled to take his eyes away.

"Did you hear? Phone."

His mother's voice was rising quicker than a Zico free kick.

"All right Mum, I'm coming."

He galloped down the stairs, ignoring his brother playing Scramble on the Commodore. Martin worried his brother was turning into one of those computer geeks.

"I ain't your secretary," she said.

"Hello?"

"All right hero, you and Stace up for a night down the Elephant? Heard there's a new film out." said Johnny.

"What, tonight?"

"What all that success affecting your hearing is it? Of course tonight."

Martin snooped into his pocket to find the grand sum of eighty-three pence.

"Love to fella, but I'm skint."

"Find some dosh. What about the old woman?"

Martin resisted the urge to pass the phone to Rose.

"You're having a laugh. She's just forked out for a telly and some computer games for my brother. Why don't we just chill out?"

Johnny huffed in disappointment.

"Mart, show some adventure will you? How about Stace? You sure she can't sponsor you?"

Martin refused to entertain that idea.

"I ain't having my bird take me out. No, you and Trace have a blinder."

"Sure I can't change your mind?"

Martin's empty pocket reminded him of his fiscal downturn.

"Can't do it mate. To be honest I could do with a rest."

Martin's ears stung the cold plastic of the phone.

"All right mate, see you tomorrow then."

The freezing plastic was undeniable. Martin, perplexed, inspected the mouthpiece.

"Yeah, laters mate. Have a good one."

"You and Stacey be good, I won't."

The line expired with Johnny laughing into static etherealness of termination. Martin gazed at his statuette one last time before falling into a long overdue sleep.

"Catch, Wazza."

A hurled can missed the target and spluttered its guts onto the grass.

"What'd you throw it for?"

Charlie shrugged. He looked forward to a life without the presence of Mr. Harris after his expulsion.

"Ain't my fault you've got no co-ordination."

He took a hard swig from his blue can. The liquid tasted dire yet the strength of drink surged through his arteries.

"Tell you what Wazza, you can't beat this Tennant's Super, can you?"

"Give us a can and I'll let you know."

Charlie allowed the drink to wallow in his mouth before beckoning his disciple towards him.

"Don't throw it this time."

Charlie allowed himself another mouthful to inflate his cheeks and faced Warren. He pressed his palms together and emptied his mouth's contents in a lager christening spray.

His friend staggered away in disgust.

"That's out of order."

Charlie's friends burst into hysterics. Charlie hadn't laughed so much since the group stripped, tied and punched one of the eleven year olds upside down on the school railings by his underpants and belt.

"Sorry mate, couldn't resist. I bet it tastes good though?"

Charlie offered his mucous encrusted handkerchief to help clean up the mess.

"Tastes like honey. You're still a prick though."

"Charlie, it looks like someone's spunked all over his face don't it?" chirped Oscar.

Another giggling fit followed.

"Sod off, Wazza. Anyway, get this down you."

Warren wrenched the can from his leader's hand. He contemplated repeating the trick on his tormentor. One flash of Charlie's feral eyes ensured he took a prudent approach. Anyone who smashed a desk over Mr. Harris's head deserved respect.

"That's it, Warren. Can't believe you took my last can."

Warren shrugged.

"Well, get some more then. We don't need to buy so much 'cause Frankie ain't coming is he?"

"Oh him? His Mum said he can't come so he wimps out. I'm thinking of booting him, I need my boys to have a bit of bottle."

Warren eased himself away Charlie's rage. Frankie had a habit of curbing the wild boy's excesses.

"To hell with him. Here I am celebrating my release from that dump and he can't be arsed to turn up."

Charlie swigged again, emptying the contents into his gullet.

"That's five down my scrag. What'd you say we go for the record and go for six or seven?"

Warren's stomach performed a peculiar dance, but he didn't mind the vomit pools of a good night out.

"Sounds good to me. You got some dosh? I'm skint."

The slap of hand on empty pocket gave Warren his answer.

"What about you, Oscar. You flush?"

An impersonation of a limp tea pot didn't raise their capital.

"Oh well, just have to go home then." surrendered Warren.

"Wazza, Wazza, Wazza, you disappoint me son."

"What you on about? We've got no cash and we can hardly rob our own supply can we?"

Charlie nodded and pointed to Johnny and Tracey drew closer.

The two boys followed Charlie's finger to where his ex-school's striker kissed his girlfriend.

"Oi, what'd you think you're doing kissing down here? You need to ask permission mate."

Johnny flinched when something unwanted land on his shoulder. He pulled away from the delights of Tracey's lips.

"What's your game? Get your hand off me."

Baleful eyes met each other. Johnny compressed his fists. He didn't like the odds but stood his ground.

"That ain't nice. There you are kissing on my patch and you go on at me, not right at all mate."

"You get in my face again and I'm going to kick the shit out of you and your little friends."

Johnny stared into Charlie's eyes, unafraid and ready.

"Johnny, leave it, it's not worth it. Come on the bus will be here soon."

Tracey tugged on his arm yet Johnny stood resolute.

"Dunno how you can kiss him darling, not when you've got real men right in front of you."

Johnny recognised his aggressor when his right fist landed on Charlie's jaw. He knew it was the boy who had been expelled. Johnny reloaded ready to punish Charlie and his friends.

"Charlie, you all right mate?" asked Warren, who edged into the violence zone.

"You want some?"

Warren waited for Oscar to move beside him.

"Johnny, leave it, come on the bus is coming. Look."

Charlie squirmed on the floor holding his jaw. He dabbed at fresh blood, vowed revenge.

"Get him. Are you poofs or what?"

Charlie's colleagues jumped their prey. Johnny sidestepped Warren's lunge and met Oscar full on with a right cross sending him to the pavement. Warren turned to see Johnny chase him and land two heavy blows to the side of his head. A tooth escaped in a perfect arc.

"I warned you lot, didn't I? You didn't know my old man was a boxer, did you?"

Warren didn't mind knocking over eleven year olds but a fit strong youth was a step too far.

"Johnny, the bus is here," pleaded Tracey.

Her boyfriend turned his head to see their salvation squeal to a stop. Charlie dipped his hand into his inside pocket.

"Johnny, watch out."

Charlie intended to stab him between his shoulders. He didn't anticipate Johnny turning around. He didn't predict the blade piercing the soft tissue protecting his precious heart.

"Fuck, Oscar come on."

Johnny staggered in bewilderment. He blinked in disbelief at Charlie's bloodied face before flopping onto a concrete bed.

"Johnny, no!" screamed Tracey

Tracey knelt beside who she thought would have been the father of their children. His eyes lay open but didn't recognise the young girl who cradled his perfect face in his blindness.

"Someone get an ambulance. Help him, please!"

Several frantic adults joined her. The arm of a uniformed man ushered her to her feet.

"Come on love, let's get you away from this."

Tears bore panic furrows down her distorted face. She looked into the face of the conductor.

"Does anyone know first aid?" he asked.

Tracey heard the question but didn't pay heed. Johnny lay dead still.

Martin slipped the record from its flash jacket. He loved it when Mike Read dared to ban it from the Radio and ensured the record went straight to number one. He eased the spindle across and dropped the needle. He reclined and closed his eyes when Holly Johnson burst into song.

"Why you listening to this crap, Mart?"

He jumped. His best friend waited for his answer in front of the stereo.

"How'd you get in? And this is a tune and a half."

Johnny leant back on the sideboard.

"It's crap and you know it. Can't you put something a bit more soulful on."

Martin disagreed.

"You want to get yourself an education in music, John. Anyway, ain't you supposed to be with Trace?"

His friend shook his head. Martin struggled to keep himself warm.

"John? You ain't split up?"

He nodded, "In a manner of speaking, yeah, I had to go."

Martin gasped at the sight of blood on his friend's chest. It cascaded down his legs towards his trainers and onto the floor.

"Oh no. John, not you, not you mate."

"Martin, it's so cold, so bloody cold."

Martin choked when hard emotion ripped into his voice.

"No, I can't believe it. I won't believe it, if I close my eyes you'll be gone."

He closed his eyes when Holly urged him to relax. He remembered Johnny scoring the winner, picking up the shield and visualised the two of them turning out for England.

He opened his eyes. He sat alone. Martin convinced himself about misguided intuition. He'd have a long, long talk with his best friend tomorrow about the future. Frankie ended and the slow tread of static crackled back. He heard the phone ring. He let his mother answer.

Martin clutched his England top and assured himself it was Aunt Julie talking about going to bingo this weekend.

Three minutes later or was it two? His mum opened the door and stared at him with her mascara running. She shook her head before the tears descended again. She sat beside her son who wrenched his shirt into a snake of sorrow.

"Martin, I'm so sorry."

"I know Mum, I know."

He cried. The pain cut to the base of his soul. His mother hugged him and shook him back and forth as if she could soothe his torment away. His eyes slammed and deep within the cruel depths, shadows laughed.

Chapter 12 School's Out

Another one. Martin battled the vomit gurgling at the base of his throat.

"Go on, get it down you."

He knocked the drink back. His face flushed. He allowed himself an excuse of a grin.

"Not bad eh, Joey? Fourth one and I'm still standing."

Joey appraised the braggart failing in his attempts to impress. He called out to his friend.

"George, I reckon our friends ready to graduate. What'd you reckon mate?"

The eighteen-year old veteran tossed Joey a paper bag filled with golden treasure.

"Easy, you know how much this cost?"

The jangling coins reminded Joey how much state money remained. Unemployed, idle and a slave to drink. He'd never been happier.

"Sorry mate, I don't know Joey, I reckon he's going to go."

Martin gave George the thumbs' up.

"I don't know. He's almost fifteen, I reckon he's up for it. Besides, until you've spewed your guts, you can't be in with us. I'll show him how it's done."

A bottle of Teachers escaped from the bag. Joey tossed the bottle cap over his shoulder.

"Won't be needing that, will we? Here goes."

He slammed the neck of the bottle into his mouth and tilted his head back. Martin stood amazed whilst the burning liquid streamed into his drinking buddy. Joey didn't cough or splutter and licked his lips.

"Here you go, do it just like me."

Martin peered into doom in a bottle and brought it to his mouth.

"Don't forget your hygiene."

Martin shrugged. Joey shook his head.

"Wipe the top of the bottle, dummy. You don't want my germs in your gob, do you?"

He attempted to sterilise the bottle with the back of his sleeve and suckled on the glass.

"Remember, tilt your head back, swallow hard and let it in."

Martin blanched when the burning liquid scored a paralytic path into his volatile stomach. He wanted to choke but carried on swallowing. Martin ripped the bottle away from his lips and raised his hand to stem the inevitable eruption.

"Here he goes, go on Martin," cheered George. Quavers, Kestrels, Big Mac and Teachers made a new home at the bottom of his trousers and his trainers.

"Top man, top man," said Joey who surveyed the biological masterpiece with pride. Martin tried to speak yet his stomach finished the conversation.

"Another one. This is well impressive."

Martin's pyroclastic flow spluttered through the railings. He prayed no-one was winding their way up the stairs. He brushed his fingers to find a film of noxious fibre. The noisome stench prompted him to a glorious finale.

He inspected the shattered remains of his food. He hoped he hadn't spewed out a vital organ or two. He left a gruesome trail of yellow on his brow while he tried to wipe some of the copious amounts of sweat away.

A firm hand slapped his shoulder.

"You all right mate? Impressive debut, but do you want to go for the title?"

Joey took another strong dose into his throat.

"Now I'm feeling it. I'm feeling it now, George."

Joey passed the bottle to his seasoned drinking partner. He took at least three hard swallows before gasping.

"Greedy, no need for that was there?"

Joey snatched the bottle away and looked at Martin.

"Ready?"

"Ready? What'd you mean?"

Martin smelt the whiskey on Joey's breath. He took the bottle and repulsion as temptation battled in his sozzled mind. He dreamed of dismal oblivion and raised the bottle near his lips.

"You're ready to really let rip now. You've chucked up and your stomach's empty. You're ready for a proper session now."

"I can't Joey. I'm done."

"I'll tell you when you're done," chided his mentor.

"Trust me, if you join us now and it'll be Wednesday when you know where you are. Come on, try and be a man."

Martin necked another measure. His world swayed and spun ever faster. He stared at seven versions of Joey and George. He tried to understand their words yet made no sense of their laughing babble. To hell with school, football, his family and even Stacey.

Liquid spilled over his trousers. Joey ripped the bottle from Martin's grasp appalled at the waste of precious alcohol. George and Joey howled with pleasure when they addressed their recruit.

"Martin, you're well and truly pissed."

He tried to respond, his lips failed to match his thoughts.

"You what mate? You've lost me."

Martin's legs wobbled and dumped him in his own pool of vomit.

"You ain't half gonna stink. His friends' hands hoisted him up and guided him downstairs.

"Come on, let's get some air."

George decided their protégé had enough. Joey toyed with the idea of shoving more grog inside, yet even his stomach rolled over and over.

"Where'd you live?"

Uncomprehending vacant eyes rolled in their sockets oblivious to Joey's question.

"Listen, where'd you live mate?"

"On the, on the, on the essst…"

Joey slapped Martin with enough force to straighten his speech for a second or two.

"Slow down, we need you to get you home. Now where'd you live?"

"On the estate."

George clapped him on the shoulder.

"Good man."

"Here."

The female voice showed little evidence of concern.

"What?"

"On your cabinet I've put a glass of water, get it down you."

Martin's nose fought the reek of nausea. The stench of stale sick promised another outburst.

"Don't you dare. You've already spewed all over the carpet."

He didn't know how he was in his pyjamas and lying in bed. His mother guessed his thoughts.

"Couldn't even bloody dress yourself, could you? Disgusting at your age to be drunk as a skunk. You're supposed to be at school today. What are you going to say to Stacey? What are you going to do about that mess in the living room?"

Each question blasted his sensitive eardrums. His mother's voice grew ever louder.

"I ain't standing for it Martin. I didn't stand for it from your father and I'm not having it off you either. No way."

His eyes threatened to leap out of their sockets when violent light sprang into life.

"I know you've lost your best friend but this ain't the answer. It never is."

The door slammed in the frame. Martin recalled a vague memory of disgorging his stomach's contents onto an alien floor. He stretched out a trembling hand and seized the tumbler. He struggled to straighten himself in the bed before allowing a few life giving drops into his throat. He never imagined the taste of water to be so good. His throat felt as if someone had driven razors down his oesophagus. He remembered his alcoholic education with Teachers.

"Can't believe I drunk whiskey," he whispered.

He braved another swig. His insides raged with the sweet pain of raw alcohol.

"Never again, never again," he vowed under his breath.

He stumbled to the breakfast table. His milky Weetabix bore him no pleasure yet secured the lining of his stomach. He fidgeted under the constant stare of his mother. Danny maintained a watchful silence from the haven of the living room.

"What happened last night then?"

"I don't know, Mum. I didn't think I'd get in such a state."

"You're right, you didn't think did you?" snapped Rose.

Her voice trumpeted through the fragile veil of drunken serenity.

"I'm sorry," he said.

"You will be. I can promise you that. After you've got that down you, there's a nice little job in the front room. Oh yes, another thing, you can wash your own clothes today."

Martin stared down at the churned mess staring back at him from the breakfast bowl. He touched his stomach wary of another guttural explosion.

He brother sneaked into the room sporting a grin. He wanted to threaten to break his jaw yet stayed his anger.

"All right, Martin?" he said too with too much happiness.

"Not really, Dan."

Danny poured a glass of strawberry milkshake. Martin swore he clanged the spoon on the side of the glass with all the strength he possessed.

"Do you want some, Mart. It tastes really nice."

"No thanks."

A loud clattering came from the living room. His mother switched the vacuum cleaner into life. Martin brushed his brow clear of fresh sweat.

"You was so drunk last night Mart, well pissed. Bloody hilarious, especially when you spewed all over the carpet."

Bastard, thought Martin.

"Cheers Danny, really needed to know that."

His brother tilted his neck back, licked his lips clean of milkshake and offered his brother the empty glass.

"My pleasure, Mum's well hacked off with you though. I wouldn't want to be in your shoes."

His voice fell to silence when the vacuum cleaner raced across the living room. Martin stared at his unappetizing breakfast and forced himself to indulge the pleasure of another mouthful. His stomach protested but he needed food to settle him down. The nausea relented after the fourth mouthful. His head banged whilst the hammer of shame continued to beat. The vacuum cleaner fell to silence after one final sweep.

"You had any more water?" yelled Rose.

Martin shook his head. She cracked open a cupboard and dragged out a fresh glass.

"Bloody stupid kid. I bet you've got a minging headache."

"Yeah."

She slammed the water down next to his empty bowl.

"That's 'cause you're dehydrated. Get that in you and it'll help sort out your headache."

He sipped a mouthful of curative water. Rose pulled back and sat opposite. He lowered his eyes to the table under his mother's examination.

"Why, Martin? Tell me why."

Her voice softened. Martin squirmed.

"I wanted to go somewhere else, Mum. It hurts, it hurts so much inside."

Martin wiped away a tear. He cursed himself for being so weak.

"I know son, but booze wont help you."

Her voice trailed away. Rose wandered into unwanted memories and prayed he'd be strong.

"It aint fair, Mum. He was my best mate and it's the best I've felt since Johnny died."

Rose scratched her chin despairing at her son's words.

"Don't ever say that, Martin. For God's sake don't follow your father, don't go down that road."

Her words were a lash to him. The image of his father swearing and staggering across their home rushed back to him.

"I won't Mum. I swear I won't."

Rose stroked his hand. For the first time in a fortnight he raised a true smile.

"Martin, Martin, Martin. What am I going to do with you?"

The pupil brushed away a globule of mud from his sleeve.

"I come into today and hear that you've been fighting. Well, what you got to say for yourself?"

He shifted from foot to foot and stared at the headmaster seated in his throne. The teacher straightened several piles of paper on the desk for the umpteenth time.

"Sorry sir. It won't happen again."

"It certainly won't, Lowe. I know you've lost your friend but life goes on young man." snorted Mr. Ryman.

Martin looked down to a muddy pair of shoes.

"I wouldn't mind Lowe if you were a substandard student but you're superb at sport. Don't throw away such a promising career lad."

He didn't care.

"I'll try not to Mr. Ryman."

The headmaster straightened in his chair.

"Glad to hear it. However, I can't allow unwarranted violence to go unchecked."

Martin wanted to protest about Rowe's constant sniping about his dead friend.

"Sir?"

"I've no option but to suspend you for two weeks. Use this time wisely Martin before you come back to us. When you return I want that fine young man who was here only two months ago. Do that for me, do it for your family but above all Martin do it for yourself."

"I will, Sir. I'm sorry."

Mr. Ryman pointed his head towards the door.

"So am I lad, so am I."

The student escaped the sentencing chamber. He wondered if Joey and George had got their money from the social.

Chapter 13 Boys Just Want To Have Fun

"You'll get into trouble Marty, no school again?"

"What are you, George, my mum or something?"

The young man tore off the top of a golden packet.

"You want a snout?"

Martin nodded. His greedy eyes alighted on a lazy heap of blue cans.

"You're eager, ain't you? Here, catch."

Keen hands ripped back the ring pull, strong liquid coursed into Martin's body.

"That's better, I needed that especially after the grief I've had off the old woman and my bird."

Joey swigged from his own can. George pondered on what lesson he could administer.

"You know your trouble?"

"No," he replied shaking his head.

"You're under the thumb son. It's a disgrace at your age. I know you can't do much about your mum but why don't you ditch this tart of yours. You should have a bit of variety."

Martin imagined his dead friend urging him to turn away. Alcohol cured all though, it resolved his problems, healed pain and brokered no competition.

"Make you right mate. Stuff Stacey and her nagging but where are we gonna pick up some new talent?"

Joey paused whilst Martin quickened his pace to a drunken state. He approved at the hardening of his recruit's stomach lining promoting to new heights of alcohol abuse.

"Mart, I didn't think you was so green mate. Meet us here at seven and we'll be off for a party. Here, catch, you need another."

Martin threw the empty can away as though it were a spent grenade pin.

"Cheers mate."

"I tell you what though son, you want hurry up and leave school. Then you can start paying us back for all this booze you've had off us."

Martin blushed aware of the debt of his friend's generosity.

"Sorry mate, I can't do anything just yet."

"Don't worry, we know you'll see us right when you can. Go on, tuck in and enjoy," interrupted George.

"Here Mart, you ever had any sweets mate?"

Martin's eyes glazed over at George's odd question.

"Course I have. Bit of a daft question ain't it?"

Joey slapped his brow.

"Not Mars bars you prick. These ones look more like Smarties."

"What you on about? You've lost me."

"George, did you kidnap him from a church choir or something?"

"Relax Joey, he's only a sprog ain't he. Lucky, we can educate him, can't we?"

Martin stubbed out a spent cigarette.

"What you two on about?"

George pointed for Martin to sit next to him on the bottom step of Fawnway House.

"You like your Tennants, you like your Kestrels and you like your Scrumpy Jack don't you?"

Martin answered by taking another healthy draught.

"Course I do. What's this got to do with sweets though?"

"All in good time, all in good time," smiled George.

"Thing with booze it takes a while to get into you."

"Yeah."

George placed his own can between his legs.

"What if I told you there was a way of getting there quicker. This way's a bit pricier and you need to know a few faces but you get to heaven quick. You interested?"

"Course I am. Go on."

"Drugs, that's what I'm talking about. They're our Smarties and you can't stop moving about once you start."

Martin sipped again from his can.

"Tell you what, we'll have a word with someone who owes us a favour or two and we'll sort some out. You game?"

The acolyte wavered under the eyes of expectation.

"Course I am," he said with defiance. "Count me in."

"Good man, and I mean man because you ain't really a boy any more my son. Not for much longer."

George took a drag from his cigarette.

"Now sod off home and do yourself a favour and tell that Stacey bird of yours you don't need her. That soppy mare ruining our mate, ain't right is it Joey?"

George's partner added a sagacious nod.

"Ain't right at all, George. He'll be better off once she's well rid. Go on Mart, go home and dump her."

Martin drained his can. His friends offered no replacement.

"This is going to be so hard."

"What's hard? Tell her to go," shrugged George.

"You should be having fun not getting nailed down. Anyone would think you was thirty, not sixteen."

The youth got to his feet, resolved to obey.

"Go on get it over with and you better not tell us you ain't done it later or you can forget about furthering your education."

Martin said his farewells. He thought about the phone all the way home.

"Stace?"

"Martin, where have you been? You were supposed to come round two hours ago."

"I've been out with Joey and George. Just had a couple of jars that's all."

He blanched when Stacey sighed.

"Haven't I told you to stay away from them? They're losers Martin and you're better than that, much better than that."

Martin's mind blazed in fury.

"No they ain't. They're all right and not boring farts like the rest of the tossers we used to hang out with."

His girlfriend gasped at his diatribe.

"Don't you speak to me like that. Look, we need to sort this out."

He thanked the devil for the chance to exploit the chink of dark light.

"Stace, look there's something I need to tell you."

"What?"

He struggled to find his voice yet thirst bore no rival.

"It's over."

"Over? What's over?"

"Us, Stace. It ain't working any more is it? We're too different."

Stacey's voice crackled with emotion, Martin rubbed his eyes free of tears.

"Martin, you can't mean that. Look, we'll sort this out, you know we belong together."

"No Stace. There's nothing to say, just do one."

Martin slammed the phone down and left the receiver off the hook. He hated himself for his brutality.

"Who was you on the phone to?"

"No-one important Mum, doesn't matter," replied Martin.

His mother shook her head. She failed to force him to go to school, failed to stop his excesses despite threatening to send him to his dad.

"You been drinking yet again?"

He giggled in answer.

"For God's sake Mart. Where'd you keep getting the money from?"

"My mates look after me Mum, and stop going on will you. I've got to have fun ain't I?"

"What about the future? You've screwed up your football, what you going to do when you leave school?"

"I've already left," he joked.

"This ain't no laughing matter. You'll live on the social all your bloody life."

He reached out for his jacket.

"What's wrong with that, Joey and George are doing it and I'm not being some slave for some fat git somewhere."

"Martin, listen to yourself."

Rose found no more tears. For the first time in years, she wished her ex-husband stood beside her. Martin never heard her any more.

"Bye."

"Where you going?"

Martin slammed the door and tottered his way to the park. The pleasant spring air helped melt the guilt. He searched his inside pocket and yanked out a pack of twenty and sparked up. The taste reminded him of his dad, yet he formed a respect for nicotine. If he got cancer, so what? He looked like an adult at least. He spat out a globule of phlegm in defiance. He tried to shrink when two young females marched in his direction.

"What's your game? Getting her all upset like that."

Martin wished for a can. He didn't need to argue with blue metal.

"How long you been together?"

Martin shrugged.

"He don't even know, Stace. What a waste of space."

"It's all right, Tracey. I just need to hear it from his own lips."

Martin examined the ash trail on the pavement. He thought the dust far more attractive than his ex-girlfriend.

"Look at me."

He kept a wall of solid indifference.

"Look at your girlfriend, you heartless bastard."

He straightened at Tracey's jibe. A solitary tear betrayed the turmoil within.

"Martin, do you want to split up from me? I know we've had our problems but we can work them out, I know we can."

Martin coughed.

"I'm sorry, Stacey."

She pleaded with her eyes. She refused to believe.

"It's over. I just don't fancy you any more," he lied.

Stacey winced. Her stomach rolled as though her boyfriend punched her. He walked into the park and didn't look back when Stacey screamed a stream of curses at him. He didn't look back when Stacey fell to her knees. It was over. Done, a man at last.

"Hurry up, soppy."

Martin stumbled forward. His pain from four hours ago lingered on the edge of oblivion.

"You've split with your bird ain't you?"

Joey nodded at the sight of the red pits under Martin's eyes.

"It's all right mate, it's tough but it had to be done. You'll thank me soon enough, especially after tonight."

Martin's mood darkened. He kidnapped a can of Kestrels.

"Get that down you. You need to lighten up before we go down Charlie's."

Martin tilted his head back, curious about the venue they were heading for.

"Who's Charlie?"

George laughed.

"You ain't heard of Charlie? He's a top geezer Marty, he'll sort you out, I promise."

The trio walk towards Camberwell. Martin seized another can.

"Here we go, let the fun begin," beamed Joey.

The young adventurer stood before a set of old flats. His companions took the stairs and ignored the unreliable lift.

"Aint going in there mate, got stuck in there for four hours the other week. You need to go for a slash?" asked George who urinated in the stairwell.

"Think I will as it happens."

The trio expelled the remnants of lager. A middle aged bespectacled owl edged past in disgust.

"Terrible, you bloody yobs shouldn't be allowed out."

Joey and George turned with their trousers hugging their ankles.

"What, ain't you ever seen a pair of pricks before?"

The man scuttled off and the three youths had never laughed so hard.

"I'll report you." lied the tenant.

"Go and get a life you sad git. Come on Martin, let's find Charlie."

They climbed several flights of stairs until they reached the seventh floor. Heavy reggae music throbbed from the end of the balcony.

"Charlie?"

"Wow, what a genius you are," joked Joey, "course it is."

Joey thumped the door. He heard nothing except the sound of heavy beats.

"Hold on a minute."

Joey bent over and peered through the rusty letterbox. Several shapes danced to and fro in the passageway.

"Oi, let us in people."

The fake emerald painted door yielded. The trio entered the flat to the tunes of Paul Blake and the Bloodfire Posse.

"All right Charlie, good to see you mate."

Charlie hugged Joey, shook his hand.

"Good to see you and you, George."

He repeated the gesture, turned his attention to Martin.

"Who the new boy then?"

"Martin. My name's Martin Lowe."

Charlie laughed and embraced his visitor.

"He's all right Charlie, he's a bit naive and we thought you could help us in his education." said Joey.

The dread-locked figure bobbed his head in approval.

"You want something to drink?"

Martin pined for another hit of lager yet Joey intervened.

"We've done that Chas. We were hoping for something stronger, if you know what I mean."

Joey flashed a twenty under Charlie's nose.

"Best you step into my office then."

Martin went to follow the two men to a small pale door.

"Are you a battyman or something? Just wait outside," ordered their host.

Martin thanked the dark light for hiding his embarrassment. He winced when he received a slap to the back of his neck.

"You muppet. You don't go in there unless you're holding folding."

George turned his attention to a vixen who sidled beside him. Her pair of black thigh length boots shined a perfect reflection of the flat. George sighed at the sight of her bare thighs beneath a flimsy flamingo dress. She caressed his face with a velvet glove.

"Bit overdressed ain't you boys? Let me take your coats. I'm Amy."

The music pounded ever louder. The usherette eased George's jacket from his shoulders before flicking open a bathroom door with the heel of her boot. She hurled the jackets into the bath. She breezed close to Martin and dismissed a look of disapproval at George.

"Does his mum know he is out? I don't know if we've got any lemonade or jelly for your boy."

"He's all right Amy. He's just split up with his bird."

Martin trailed his eyes to the top of Amy's thighs. Amy giggled at the thought of him naked.

"S'pose as long as it works, he'll do."

She trailed long fingers across his chest and pressed herself tight against him satisfied when he responded.

"Well, you going to stay here all night or you going to get friendly on the dance floor. I'll even help sort your little mate out."

George nodded.

"Love to Ames, but my mate's in with Charlie. Need a little boost to keep myself going."

She snaked across the passageway and opened the door to the heavy reggae beat.

"See me inside when you're ready. The music will get quicker, much quicker, laters."

She vanished. Martin squirmed to dissipate the interest growing in his legs.

"Hands off Marty, Amy's mine. Save your hard on for someone else."

The toilet door swung open. Joey and Charlie exchanged handshakes.

"Pleasure doing business with you, Joey. Now enjoy and don't forget to get some water from the kitchen."

Charlie disappeared back into the crowded living room.

"Here we go boys, come on, let's get on it."

Joey handed Martin a small packet of round pills.

"Just take one at a time. I don't want to be running you to hospital or worse, do I?"

George presented the pair with a couple of dirty tumblers. The huge grin on his face informed Joey he'd already taken.

"Bottom's up, Marty boy."

Joey placed the pill on his tongue and swallowed hard from the glass. He indicated for Martin to follow.

"I'm looking for Amy. Catch you lot later," interrupted George.

Martin balanced the tiny pill on his it on his tongue. He swallowed and waited for the world to spin.

"Come on, follow me and party." roared Joey.

The pair barged into the living room where the bass thrummed with divine might. Martin struggled to focus on the music, bodies pressed hard against him. He looked for his friends yet floundered in a lake of strangers.

All that mattered was the music, the beat and the urge to move. The tempo pushed and Reggae surrendered to House. Martin grinned with lunacy and burst into dance moves he never knew. A blonde girl and her jet haired friend moved next to him. They encircled Martin and applauded when he danced ever faster. The light-haired girl moved her right leg inside his and answered

Martin's wild leer with one of her own. She clasped her left leg to his posterior and drew him close.

"You can have me, you know you want to," she ordered.

Her hands parted his zip and drew him outside. Martin dug into velvet flesh when she thrust him inwards. Bystanders cheered and indulged in their own acts of frantic lovemaking. She pulsed again and again. Martin exploded. She released him and laughed to the sun in the lone light bulb.

"I want some of that. Give him here."

Her friend clasped her hands across Martin's shoulders before crossing her legs behind the small of his thighs, entrapping him and letting him bear her weight.

"My turn." she said.

Martin responded in a new cycle of lovemaking. All around him lay chaos. His eyes glazed in pure delirium.

"Are we having fun? Everyone getting high yet?" yelled the M.C.

A hail of approval answered. The nameless girl decamped, composed her clothing before kissing him.

"Thanks love, I won't forget you in a hurry," she said before vanishing into the throng. Martin looked for her friend and found her performing another amorous jig around another raver.

Martin's world slowed. His body lurched into inertia, his mind begged for more.

"All right son, look at you," laughed Joey when he pointed towards the top of Martin's jeans.

"Your strides mate, come on, you better follow me."

He followed Joey away from the debauched dance floor. A pair of lovers leered, blew a kiss and he declined the offer to join them.

"Come on spunky, let's get you in the bathroom," urged his guide.

"Where's George?"

"He's with some brass called Amy. Still at it when I left him. Anyway, you still feeling good?"

Martin shook his head.

"No mate. My legs are stiffening, everything seems so slow."

Joey pushed the bathroom door open and persuaded two men kissing to leave.

"You need another boost that's all. Anyway, get that cloth over there and clean up."

Martin moistened the tip of the towel under the tap before wiping up as best he could.

"Those men, they were kissing."

"Why, you looking to get involved? I'll call them back if you like."

Martin whitened.

"I'm not like that."

His partner ordered him to take another pill.

"You need to broaden your mind. You never know until you try. Get that down you."

Martin let the used towel fall to the floor.

"I hope Charlie don't mind, Joey. I mean, it's a bit out of order ain't it?"

"Don't worry about it. He's making a fortune tonight."

He darted over to the sink.

"You could have warned me.'

"Leave it alone soppy. Get your arse in the kitchen and swallow."

The two men outside returned to their love nest. Martin pressed another tablet into his mouth and waited for the magic to begin once more.

"Good?"

"Let's get out there." said Martin.

He didn't need more sex. Martin yearned to move, dance and catch every beat. George called him over gave his protégé a huge hug.

"All right stud. Good to see you getting in the spirit of things."

They edged closer to the speakers. Martin explored every fibre in the carpet beneath his toes, the fake glitter-ball presented him with the image of a hundred thousand bodies dancing and thrashing together. The wild wind gathered him and whipped his body to greater frenzy. He looked to the metal can in his hand and delighted at the presence of a familiar friend.

He tilted his head back and allowed the drug to mix with strong lager. He floated ever higher. The chemical war with alcohol in his body escaped in pressing streams of sweat. He wanted to stay forever.

They left at seven A.M., exhausted, dehydrated and elated.

Chapter 14 Passing Out

The time for Martin to finalise his life arrived. He glanced at the timetable: maths first, geography and then woodwork.

"Good luck, son."

He received a kiss from his mother and returned the compliment.

"Thanks Mum. I'll see you later."

Martin hadn't a clue about what answers to write. He turned up at several mock exams and the highest score he registered amounted to twenty-eight percent in English. He turned his thoughts to the week after when school disappeared into history.

He kept away from his ex-school friends and absorbed the icy glares from Tracey when she shielded his ex-girlfriend from his presence. Tracey detested the sight of him although he took heart when his first love rewarded him with a smile.

Martin played with a plastic pouch of his favourite sweets in his pocket. He wondered what the teachers would make of a pupil standing on the desk and dancing on the exam papers.

He strutted to the third aisle and took the ninth seat of twenty. A stern looking Mr. Hague patrolled the large desk at the front and fumed whilst tardy pupils settled. The maths teacher glanced towards the clock.

"Good morning. Thank you for coming, now if you could be so kind as to give me some quiet."

The nervous chattering continued whilst lives and careers prepared to be made or broken.

"Quiet," roared Mr. Harris and silence reigned. Mr. Hague thanked his colleague.

"Right, I'll try not to keep you long but there are a few things I need to run over with you all."

He scoured the hall to catch anyone not paying attention.

"Make no bones about this ladies and gentlemen, today is one of the most important days of your lives. Today, you put into practice all what you've learned in those lessons of yours, assuming you've been paying attention of course."

He waited for laughter. No-one but a few teachers showed amusement.

"The first exam you will take is mathematics. Observe the time limit and you will be permitted to use calculators. However, certain questions will require you to show powers of logic as you reach the solution."

A few faces exchanged confused looks.

"In other words, show your sums, not just the answer."

The martinet folded his arms, inhaled deep.

"I'm sure I don't need to remind you that there is to be absolutely no talking. If I or any of my colleagues catch anybody in any form of communication, both, and I stress both, parties will be ejected from the exam and be marked as a failure. If anyone needs the toilet or has some other issue then they are to raise their hand until one of us sees you."

Martin picked up his pen and scribbled his name on the desk next to someone called Casey.

"Please ensure that you write your name in capitals in the appropriate box."

The teacher inspected his watch.

"All that remains for me is to wish you good luck and do your best. You may begin."

Martin glanced towards the test paper and entered his name. He turned the page and despaired when he saw the word logarithm. He never understood this pointless drivel when he was in class but now it may as well have been written in Cyrillic. He grabbed the spare piece of paper and drew a few circles; he wished it was an art exam. Seconds elapsed into minutes and the first hour passed. Martin attempted seven questions. He straightened his paper and raised his arm.

"Yes, Lowe. What can I do for you?" enquired an official.

"Miss Garvey, I'm done. Can I go now?"

She flinched at the request.

"You sure? Martin, perhaps you can use the rest of the time to make sure you've answered the questions to the best of your ability."

He eased the chair away from the desk.

"There's no need. I've done all that, it's as good as it's going to get."

She pointed towards the main desk.

"If you're sure Martin, if you're absolutely sure, you can go."

He escaped and giggled amidst the song of gasps from his astonished fellow pupils.

"Cheers Miss. I'll be back at two then."

He presented the paper towards a doubtful Mr. Hague. He said nothing except thank you and good luck.

Martin followed the same procedure for each of his seven exams. Each time the same astonished looks met his departure. He didn't care. Freedom waited. He looked forward to having money and being out of this pointless institution.

He sighed when Mr. Harris ignored him when he left the exam hall for the last time. He knew his former favourite teacher thought 'waste of talent, waste of a life.' He chanted again the mantra he began after Johnny's unwarranted death; "fuck football."

"All done?"

Martin grabbed a Kestrels.

"Sure is mate. No more exams, no more school." he yelled.

His scream thrilled his two drinking partners. Several tenants stared with poisonous eyes at the trio.

"Top man, course, you know what this means don't you?"

Joey rolled out a ten pound note onto his palm.

"Means your unemployed mate and you get paid by the government. Only thing Thatcher's good for 'cause you got zero chance of getting a job."

Joey pointed in the direction of the examination hall.

"Thing is Mart, you're the smart one, not those bookworms who think a silly little certificate is going to make a difference."

Joey and George nodded whilst they listened to their guru.

"Bet you they'll be drawing money like the rest of us. A couple might learn to make a cup of tea or two but they just don't see it. Careers? It's all cobblers and I should know."

"How many exams did you pass then, Joey?" asked George who had been intrigued by his friend's unexpected revelation.

"The works mate. English, CSE 1, Maths CSE 2, Geography 2, Biology 2, Woodwork 1, Economics 1 and Art 4. I only got 4 in Art because the teacher was a waster."

Martin shook his head at the revelation. He imagined Joey hadn't bothered with exams.

"Joey, you're bloody Einstein. How comes you didn't get a job or go to college or something?"

Joey allowed the lager fog to lift for a second. He recalled the thrill of his first job interview and the ill-fitting suit he wore. He remembered the polite smile from the receptionist, the protocol he followed to the letter when he discussed the possibility of becoming a filing clerk. He remembered the joy when he ripped open the envelope from J.M. Press a week later.

Thank you for your application for the position of Filing Clerk with our organisation. Unfortunately, on this occasion you have not been successful in your application as we were looking for someone with more experience.

Once again, we would like to thank you for expressing an interest in the position and we will retain your details on file.

Yours sincerely

He gave up after several more rejections. His friends drugs and alcohol enabled him the thrill of life.

"Joey?"

"Sorry mate, miles away. In answer to your question grasshopper, I did and you know what they all said to me?"

Martin shrugged.

"They told me no chance. Not interested in a spotty sprog like you, well, that was it for me."

He took a hard swig from his can.

"Like I said, those sops coming out of school don't know what's coming. Haven't got a clue have they, George?"

George agreed and stared at the ground. He never ever made it to the interview stage.

"Anyway, that's enough of this old pony. You're free Marty boy, time to celebrate I'd say."

Martin accepted the gift of a small P.V.C packet in his left fist.

"A special gift from Charlie for your graduation day. Go on, you deserve it.'

Martin glanced around.

"What here? In public?"

Joey flicked his wrist as if to swat away invisible flies.

"Don't worry about the residents. They don't give a toss about us as long as we don't interfere with them. And if we do, they can't do fuck all about it."

"Just pop them."

Martin placed one in his mouth before taking another swig from his can. Lager and chemicals hurled themselves into his stomach before hurling him into oblivion.

Life became a whirlwind. Thursday became a sacred day when he received the treasured giro. Joey and George made sure the cash never lasted long. They made a point of reminding him of the debt. He knew it'd be a while before he'd be square. He never gave thought to cash though, it was all booze, drugs and sex. He didn't care what order life's pleasures came in.

"You up for it tonight, Mart?"

"What you got lined up, Joey?"

His friend shrugged.

"Time to raid the offy and get pissed, get juiced and get laid. Thought you'd know the drill by now, sunbeam."

George, did his nodding dog routine. Martin wondered what would happen to him if Joey ever moved on.

"I do mate, I just thought we might do something a bit different that's all. Two years I've been knocking around with you lot. I ain't being funny Joey but I'm getting bored with it. I've had enough of those idiots down the social looking all snooty at me and asking me what jobs I've applied for, seeing me as some piece of trash."

George whistled a tune.

"George, can't you come up with something better than that? Rick Astley, you're having a giraffe mate."

He claimed silence under Joey's verbal barrage and lit up another nicotine stick.

"You know your trouble, Mart?"

"Yes I do. Hanging around with you wasters."

Joey punched Martin's arm in jest.

"Who you calling a waster? That's gratitude for you, all that sponsoring we did, saving you from some soppy bird and introducing you to the finer things of life and you call me a waster. Mart, that hurts."

Stacey's spectre haunted his thoughts at Joey's flippant aside. He wondered where she was, who she was with.

"I know what you need, Mart. Excitement. This ain't enough for you any more, you need something a bit more pokey than sweeties don't you?"

"What you suggesting?"

"Something more refined. Trouble is it's a bit pricey Mart, but the buzz is awesome."

Martin snatched a cigarette from George and inhaled a lungful of healthy fumes.

"How much we talking then?"

"Three weeks' dole and that's just for one session. Tell you what though if I get some, you and George can sub me back over the next couple of months."

The small gang agreed. Martin approved and yearned for a change.

"What about the old woman, Mart? She getting on your case?"

Martin discharged a cloud of phlegm onto the pavement enjoying the jellied pattern it made for him.

"Always mate, to be honest though I think she's giving up on me. Keeps telling me I'll be packed off to the old man but that won't happen."

"How can you be so sure?" asked George.

Martin laughed.

"It's obvious mate. As much as she hates what I do, she hates that old tosser even more. I ain't seen the old bastard in over twelve years now. If I never see him again it'll be too soon."

The duo were taken aback by Martin's tirade.

"Blimey mate, he must have pissed you off something cruel. What'd he do to you?"

"Knocked the old woman about, knocked me and my brother about and was always pissed. The man's a loser."

Martin hurled an empty can into the wall opposite savouring the rattle when it nestled by a pile of crisp packets.

"Nothing wrong with getting pissed Mart, I'd say you was following in his footsteps mate."

Joey's words bit deep. The drunkard's son grabbed his tormentor by the lapels of his jacket.

"Don't you ever say that. Don't ever say that or I'll swear Joey, I'll do you."

George grabbed at Martin's wrists yet failed to break his demonic grip.

"Don't ever say his name again. Don't even think about him, just let me be."

"All right mate, calm down. I didn't know, did I?"

Joey's reason swept Martin's rage aside. George barged him away from a shocked Joey.

"Come on mate, have another one of these. Joey didn't mean anything by that did he?"

Martin nodded, accepted the amnesia of alcohol.

"I shouldn't have freaked out but the thought of that man makes my blood boil."

Joey sidled round Martin before offering his hand.

"I'm sorry Mart, I was bang out of order mate."

Martin took the peace offering and manufactured a sad smile.

"You weren't to know. I shouldn't have lost it. I'm sorry for being a dick."

Joey swigged on his can.

"Don't worry. Anyways, done now and I'm going to sort out that business I was on about. Meet me at my flat at eight."

"Laters Joey. I'm going to have a lay down, getting a banging headache."

They parted. Martin, for once, helped his mother back at home.

"Come in, come on into my little world."

Joey's world consisted of one distressed bed, a silver buttoned television sitting on the edge of a tiny sideboard, a cheap cabinet stuffed with jumbled clothes sat to Martin's left and the final addition a Technics turntable. Martin inhaled the stench of herbs.

"You still smoking that crap, Joey?"

"Hark at Ironman over there. Course I am Mart, helps me chill, don't it?"

Martin sighed. He tried weed several times and it just made him giggle.

"Does nothing for me. How'd you get on?"

Joey patted his bed and told George to close the door.

"Get down here and you can find out."

Joey pulled out a small packet of white dust.

"Good quality this is. Just wait until you try it."

Joey placed a piece of paper next to his television and made three almost straight lines. He licked his lips and imagined the dust ripping up his brain.

"Martin, seeing as you're new to this, you can do the honours."

The old teenager stooped over the first line and lowered his head towards the forbidden treasure.

"You snort it straight up your hooter. That's it, good job."

Martin reeled when the drug jackbooted its way through his left nostril. He departed the realm of lucidity and the world swam in dizzy hurricanes. He sat on the bed and giggled when George took his fill. Soon all three babbled nonsense to each other and still they laughed.

Martin laid back and his eyes were pressed shut when the drug coated his neural cortex with visions of weariness. His eyes flickered to see his hands dancing a tune on their own volition. He loved not being himself and floated to see the world from elsewhere.

He looked left, right, up and down and it was just the three of them indulging the bliss of cocaine, just the three of them and the small gang of shades who watched from beyond the door.

Martin opened his eyes in panic. He hadn't seen the shades for several years and despite his catatonic state, he shivered in fear. His friends continued to laugh, disjointed from the world. Martin stormed to the door with his fist raised. Martin threw a punch at a shadow yet hit nothing but the dark fog of dismay.

Martin stood alone and heard shredded laughter leaping into the darkness beyond.

"Oi, soppy, where'd you think you're going? Get back in here and score another line."

Joey's words soothed ethereal panic. The cure of fresh oblivion too good to turn down. He fled the shades and indulged once more in sweet destruction.

Chapter 15 Cashflow

"Oi, you getting up today or what?"

Martin scrabbled for a glass of water. His throat hummed with volcano and ash, the liquid doing nothing to abate a dead desert of thirst.

"What time is it?" he croaked.

"Time you was up. Just because you're too bloody lazy to get a job doesn't mean you can sit on your arse all day."

Martin slung on his clothes. His mother rattled off a string of chores for him. He missed his friends Joey and George. Six months they'd been in work. Joey became what he swore he'd never be; an office lackey. George haunted Joey's path and grabbed a job in some grotty café. They dropped him into the shadows of a forgotten friend in one swift phone call of dismissal. Joey took on new responsibilities and the fresh clean cash in his hand every Thursday defeated his urge to self-destruct. He met with a girl from the office called Sally, the rebel fell to defeat, crushed under the heel of a stiletto.

"Oi, dreamboat get a move on."

Martin new found sobriety washed away those welcome moments of fatal fantasy. His days of humdrum boredom of watching pointless chat shows and listening to his brother who passed his exams, winning a place at college, ticked each day of the calendar with the cold shadows of unwelcome maturity.

"What you going to do with yourself today then?" asked his mother when he wrenched out a packet of Frosties.

"Dunno. Get my money and go down the park I s'pose."

"You bloody ain't. You can get yourself back here and help me with the washing for a start. There's plenty of things that need doing."

"Oh come off it, Mum. That's women's work and I've got other things to do."

Rose's eyes flared with over-ripe impatience.

"I won't come off it. You sit here all day doing sod all and you expect me to sweep up after you. I've got one word for you, Sonny Jim."

Martin swore his hearing grew more sensitive by the day. The constant recoil in his eardrums reminded him of his mother's mighty voice.

"Bollocks. If you got off your arse and got a job it might be different, but under my roof, it's my rules boy and you don't like it get out the door and see your dad."

For a moment the thought of peace and quiet of Hythe appealed. The sea air, wind of the coast and one waste of space of a deadbeat father. His mother never raised a hand, just gave him a headache.

"All right, I get the message, Mum. I'll help out when I get back."

A sigh answered. He slipped on a pair of trainers and the phone rang.

"Hello Jim. How are you?"

Another one of his mother's brothers. Uncle Jim liked to give Martin a sneaky fiver when he bumped into him.

"Yeah, he's here. I'll just get him, Martin, your uncle wants a word."

He shuddered at the sound of his name and swore his mother found an extra octave or two.

"All right there, Marty? How's it going mate?"

"Boring, Uncle Jim. There's nothing to do all day."

Rose's eyes bored into him when he recalled her orders regarding the laundry.

"I can imagine, son. I was the same at your age but you know what you need don't you?"

"Pools win would be nice Unc."

Metallic laughter pealed down the line.

"Can't argue with you there, Martin. I was thinking something a bit more practical though."

"Like what?"

Martin's brow leaked in hope at the thought of a great revelation.

"How about a job?"

Martin vowed a year ago to stay on the rock and roll. His tiny stash from the state passed to his keeper in his role as menial slave.

"Job? What is it?"

His mother stopped washing up at the distant promise of extra cash for the household.

"Driver's mate. A piece of piss Mart, and just what you need. Money ain't bad and it'll get you fit. I mean, a boy of your age shouldn't be carrying a spare tyre."

Martin's mind span in a moment of clarity.

"How much a week and how long?"

"I think it's about ninety sovs for the first three months before it goes up to one twenty. Three months after that it goes up to one fifty and if you fit in all right, they'll even help you learn to drive. There's always overtime too if you want it."

Martin found no words. His potential rise in income staggered him, he already wondered what to treat himself with.

"Well, what'd you say?"

"I'd be a mug not to."

He didn't look behind but he sensed his mother bursting with relief. He could almost hear her thoughts screaming 'at last.'

"Good man. Listen, I'll have a word with Mr. Williams and see if we can get you started on Monday. Soon as I know for sure I'll let you know so you can get onto the social."

"That's great, and Unc?"

"Yes son."

"Thanks a million. Thanks a lot."

His uncle laughed.

"Thanks he says. You won't be thanking me when I get you loading up and emptying my lorry. Put your mother on and get yourself busy round that house of yours."

"No probs."

His mother hugged him as she passed with happy tears streaming down her flushed cheeks.

"The job's a piece of piss, son. You listen to your uncle here and you'll do fine. However, if you muck him or me about and I'll get one of Maggie's millions to fill your boots. That clear?"

Martin bobbed his head in obedience whilst the steel haired disciplinarian laid out more of his duties.

"You normally do about ten to twenty drops a day, depending on how busy we are. If we're really up against it, it has been known to go up to forty, but that's normally at Christmas and there's loads of overtime then."

Martin straightened his ill-fitting grey and blue overall.

"That's not to say it's an excuse for you to hang it out. Your uncle won't let that happen but if I catch any rumour of any of my shift poncing around in cafés, pubs or sitting on their arses, it's bye bye employment."

Mr. Yorke slammed his hands together.

"That won't happen, boss. I'll keep my eye on him."

The handlebar moustached controller sipped from a polystyrene cup filled with blistering liquid disguising itself as coffee.

"Keep two eyes on him, Jim. The youth today are lazy little gits."

Martin inhaled the sharp sent of diesel. His uncle led him to the realm of honest toil.

"Come on son, you and me have got a lorry to load."

Jim led his charge to a raised platform and shook his head.

"What a bunch of wankers. I ain't having this."

Martin looked in confusion at a gathering of vehicles with several pallets before them. He pursued his uncle who disappeared through a plastic curtain. The driver paused before a battered red door before knocking.

"Come in," replied a shifty voice.

"Hello Reg, listen mate, I've got to make a complaint."

Reg rolled his eyes to a dimmed light bulb.

"Jim, ain't I got enough on my plate? Oh, is this your new helper?"

Martin examined the green stained concrete at his feet.

"Yep, he's my nephew. Martin, this here's Reggie Leonard."

Martin's hand vanished into Reggie's nicotine stained wrinkled hand.

"Good to have you aboard, Mart. Listen to your uncle and you won't go wrong."

Jim whistled whilst his foot beat a rhythm of impatience on concrete.

"I've still got a problem, Reg. The idiots on night shift have put all the light stuff to the front and the heavy gear to the back of the loading bay. They keep doing this Reg, and it ain't on."

The transport manager presented the palms of his hands in sympathy.

"I hear what you're saying, Reg. You're right, it's out of order. Trouble is my hands are tied mate if Johnny on nights don't keep his boys in order."

Jim sighed.

"So what am I supposed to do now, Reg? It takes ages to put things in the right order."

Reggie rolled his neck to the flickering fluorescent light entertaining a witless fly.

"You'll have to make do Jim, I aint got anyone spare at the moment. The boys on days are unloading and that's going to take an hour at least. I'd help myself, but I'm swamped in paperwork mate."

Jim shook his head.

"Come on Martin, welcome to Journey's End Distribution."

The manager offered a comfort of hope.

"I tell you what Jim, I'll have a word with the governor and get him to give Johnny a bollocking. I guarantee a memo to all staff will be sent out."

The duo walked away from the shadow of empty promises.

"That's all that nob's good for, bloody memos."

Jim pointed at a large open shutter with the number eight fading into a six.

"That's our baby and see all that crap in front?"

Martin nodded.

"It's all got to go on board. Now you know why I was having a whinge."

Martin's realization dawned when he spotted large heavy parcels wedged behind a host of smaller ones.

"Get yourself a pump truck from over there and we'll get this sorted."

Martin grabbed an olive truck. He winced when the wheels grated and shrieked when he guided it onto the loading bay.

"God's sake, couldn't you have got a better one than that?" groaned his uncle.

Martin glanced at the miniature car park and volunteered to change the faulty loader.

"No time for that now, son. Drag that pallet at the back to one side and put it over there on the left."

Martin nodded before slamming the wagon between the pallet. He pulled it out and the pallet stayed where it was.

"What are you doing?"

Martin repeated the process. He looked at the forks, the pallet and at the handle looking to solve the riddle of manual handling.

"Pump it up, dopey! That's why they're called pump trucks."

Jim closed his eyes and drew in a couple of lungfuls of air.

"Like this?" enquired Martin when he discovered the joy of hydraulics.

"That's it, all right, don't keep going up."

Martin tugged the pallet towards him. The pallet yielded to his instruction before toppling and sending the contents across the floor.

"Oh for fuck's sake," roared his uncle.

Martin, crestfallen, tried to apologise.

"It's not your fault son, it's those morons who loaded the pallets. They've stuck all the heavy crap on one side."

Jim helped his nephew re-stack the pallet. Mr. Yorke thundered down from the top of the loading ramp. He shook his head and pointed to the van.

"Why aint on the road yet? Stop hanging it out and get going."

Mr. Yorke didn't dally to argue when he stared into Jim's flustered face.

"Don't blame me. It's those useless loaders you employ. Maybe you want to help us load up, if you're that bothered."

The controller shuffled away back to his office mumbling words of customer dissatisfaction.

"One word of advice, Mart. Don't take any notice of managers or supervisors. They're all clueless and they're only in the jobs they do now 'cause they were rubbish on the road or the warehouse."

Martin picked up a box. His slender arms remained rooted by the sides of the potent parcel.

"How can something so small weigh so much?"

Jim laughed and pointed for Martin to place the parcel on the left side of the pallet.

"Because you ain't got any muscles yet, lanky. Don't worry, a month or two of this and you'll have bumps in places you didn't even know you had."

Jim took the parcel away from Martin and with no effort placed it in the correct spot.

"Easy, ain't it? Now come on, let's get this mess sorted out."

Jim loaded the lorry in a blur, much to Martin's astonishment. His biceps groaned whilst his uncle nodded in approval.

"What's the matter son, feeling a bit tender?"

"Just a bit. Nothing too bad though."

"You won't say that tomorrow morning, matey. Right, have a butcher's at this."

He led Martin to a clipboard stuffed with several sheets of white printer paper.

"This here's our manifest. On each line is the order in which we have to drop of the parcels. Now you know why I had you packing in a certain way."

He thought his uncle was developing the first strains of madness when he insisted a tiny aisle be set down the back of the vehicle.

"The printout shows the address of each customer and how many parcels they're getting. You get to see the same customers most of the time but occasionally we get a couple of strange ones."

He handed the important paper to Martin with reverence.

"Always remember to get the customer to sign and print his name. You do get them trying it on at times. Who do you suppose is the first one security go looking for when something goes missing?"

Martin paused while his uncle waited to see if any of his sister's intelligence had filtered down to her addled offspring.

"I guess it's the driver and his mate?"

A deep nod answered along with the words, "Bingo, I've had old D.I. Culverton on my case plenty of times I can tell you. 'Course, it's never the customer that's on the take is it?"

Martin frowned at the thought of being called a thief.

"You'll meet Culverton at some point no doubt. He's a typical failed copper who's watched too much Dempsey and Makepeace. He looks just like Chisholm on Minder. Only thing is Chisholm's smarter."

His protégé laughed at the thought of his uncle being some kind of Arthur Daley figure.

"Anyway, like I says, always get a signature, time and their name in print and they can't touch you. Right, read out the first name on that list of ours."

Martin scrolled his index finger down the page.

"J.Q.L. Records, 22 Brookmead Road and four parcels."

His uncle blipped the throttle.

"Sounds good to me, son. Best we get going or Beaky will be on our case again."

"Beaky?" asked Martin with squinted eyes.

"Is your brain still half a kip? Didn't you notice the big red hooter on old Mr. Yorke?"

Martin imagined the grumpy boss with a parrot beak before he burst into a fit of laughter.

"That's funny, Unc, Beaky!"

His laughed inside at how furious Mr. Yorke would be if he ever discovered his nickname.

"All right son, calm down and do me a favour, whilst we're at work, just call me plain old Jim. Last thing I need is having the rise taken out of me because of you being my nephew."

Martin agreed in a nod of relief. Saying uncle all day didn't befit the image of a driver's mate.

"Jim it is then. You better not tell Rose though."

Jim rewarded Martin with a slap around the back of the head.

"Oi, less of your lip or I'll have a word with your mum and you know you don't want that. Which reminds me, you only call me Jim at work. Your mother would throw a right old strop otherwise."

The lorry pulled up at a red barrier. The driver flashed his pass at the security man.

"Morning Fred, who you got in there today?"

A shiny dome reflected back from the hut's interior before adding the words, "Miss June today, Jim. You could lose yourself in there I tell you and she's got tits to die for."

The security guard straightened when Martin waved from the passenger seat.

"Who's the sprog? Ain't your love-child, is he?"

"Close," laughed Jim, "Fred, meet Martin Lowe, my nephew and as of today, my driver's mate."

Fred's eyes widened in surprise.

"What, they finally got someone to help you? Took them long enough didn't it? How long since Tony got the tin tack?"

"Three months and right on top of Christmas. Our bosses are such a nice bunch eh?"

Martin shrunk into his chair and inspected his watch. He longed to be on the road.

"Your boy's keen, I see. Better watch yourself out there when you have your extended lunch old boy."

"He'll do as he's told, Fred. Oi, and what's this about extended lunch you cheeky sod?"

The security guard raised the barrier when an impatient Capri snuggled behind Jim's lorry.

"Yeah, right, enjoy your day son and don't let the lazy git make you do all the work. See you later."

The seven and a half tonner screamed into the High Street and battled its way into the web of heavy traffic.

"One thing I'll tell you now Mart, we'll meet all sorts of drivers."

Jim pointed at a brown mini hanging several yards behind the bus in front.

"You take that one. Look, typical batty bird who ain't got a clue. Take it from me there's plenty of others like this old tart."

Jim poked his head out of the driver's window.

"Oi, keep up, will you? Some of us have got a job to do."

The woman in front smiled and waved in apology, inched closer to the bus in front allowing Jim to pull out.

"See, a few words and I can get down this road now."

Jim zipped forward, forcing the cars on the other side of the road to let him through.

"Blooming shit for brains, it does my head in when they block the road off."

A reluctant Fiat yielded to Jim's protestations and the lorry accelerated. Martin reckoned his uncle could beat his record on Pole Position in the arcade.

"Relax son, I've been doing this for over twenty years. Oi, look where you're going dopey bollocks."

Martin acclimatised to his uncle's sudden bouts of invectives when another human dared to interfere with their journey.

"Jim, Mum would have a fit if she heard you going on like that. You always seem so calm to me."

The driver laughed and swung his van through the back streets. They edged closer to his first drop point.

"I am calm, lad. I guarantee you this though, you put any man behind the wheel of a motor and things become different. You'll see for yourself one day."

Martin shook his head.

"Won't happen."

Jim snorted at his nephew's misplaced honesty.

"I bet within a couple of weeks you'll be just like the rest of us."

Martin glanced to his left when a red transit began a hazardous reversal.

"It won't happen because I'm not going to drive. Never."

A dirty brick building loomed ever closer, Jim slowed.

"You'll change your mind. All that freedom and independence, Mart? You'll learn to drive mate. I mean how are you going to take out your girlfriend or wife?"

"I ain't got one. Besides if I ever did, she could learn how to drive the motor, not me."

"You make me laugh son. Still, you might have something in getting your bird to drive you about. Maybe you're not as green as you are cabbage looking."

Martin laughed and shook his head.

"Are you saying I look stupid?"

The lorry stopped, Jim eased on the handbrake.

"All I need to say to you is pump truck. Anyway, that's enough of your old pony, time to turn those little bumps on your arms you call muscles into gear."

Martin cursed, left the cabin and helped his uncle open the shutter. He thought of pay, money and something elusive. Freedom.

Chapter 16 Journey To Hell

"I'm off to work, Mum."

Rose looked to the living room thinking it hadn't been so tidy for at least a year or two.

"All right, son. You're off out tonight ain't you?"

"Yep, off to see Joey and George remember? I ain't seen them for about four years now, should be good to see how they're getting on."

Rose wished it was a hundred years before her son met them again.

"You be careful. I'm proud of the way you turned your life around and it's no thanks to them."

He sighed.

"Mum, that was ages ago. I don't touch any of that shit now."

She handed him a packet of foil packed sandwiches.

"Yes, well you just behave yourself and watch your tongue round my house young man. You're not so big you can't get a clip round the ear."

"Leave it out, Mum. Anyway, you're too old and slow to catch me. Ouch!"

Rose tapped him on the top of his head.

"Not that slow. Now get to work."

Martin spotted a pigeon pecking at a discarded bag of chips, he wondered how many he'd chucked away in his drunken prime. His uncle pulled up and pointed to the passenger seat. He enjoyed his uncle's company yet his eyes drifted to the South London Press classifieds twice a week.

"All right, Jim."

He clambered in, Jim waved at Rose who returned his greeting.

"All right, Mart. I want a nice easy day today son, none of that cobblers like we had yesterday."

They pulled away and Martin cringed when he recalled taking out the wrong parcel for K.M.I. Products. His uncle resembled a raspberry hedgehog when he discovered Martin's faux pas. The driver's mate said a prayer of thanks when he found the parcel at a previous drop. Jim continued his diatribe when the company they had to return to was on the other side of the borough.

"It was a one off though wasn't it?"

Jim shook his head.

"Well, it was, wasn't it? I mean the amount of times I've fucked up you can count on one hand."

Jim nodded in grudging agreement.

"Maybe, but that's still too many times for my liking. You screw up and we get home late. Just you make sure you keep your eye on the ball today, especially as it's Friday."

Martin counted the cars go by. He started his own little competition to see how many red Fiestas he wracked up in a day.

"No chance of mucking up today. I'm off out with some old mates. It's blinding seeing them after all these years."

Jim snorted, in his youth he'd drink all night, ram down a curry and every now and then chuck a right hook or two.

"I can't be arsed with all that prancing about at my age. A few pints down the Green Man does me. You don't take any of those soppy drugs do you?"

Martin looked back offended.

"Course not, I'll be on the Fosters."

Jim squinted at his nephew who took a sudden undertaking of reading the latest headlines.

"Well, you just be careful. This new crap they're all taking ain't too clever. Mucks up your brain cells, not that you've got too many in that empty head of yours."

"More than you've got you old git."

Jim looked forward to the end of the day. Friday were always quiet and a time to relax.

Martin rushed to his drawer and nabbed a generous wad of ten pound notes. He recalled how Joey and George used to bail him out. The grin lessened when he remembered when they called in the debt along with copious amount of interest.

"What time you reckon you'll be back then?"

Martin threw a narcissistic stare to the youth in the mirror. The profile of a man conquering immaturity grew ever stronger.

"I don't know, Mum. You know how these things can drag on."

She folded arms and memories of vomit, atrocious singing and swearing held her attention.

"Well, give me a call if you're not coming home. I don't want to sit up all night worrying about you, do I?"

Martin exhaled a heavy gust of breath.

"Mum, for God's sake, I ain't a kid any more. Just go to bed and don't worry about me. I can take care of myself."

Martin's physique changed for the better. Years pulling and pushing heavy boxes around fulfilled his uncle's prediction of building muscles.

"I wish I had a pound for every time I've heard that over the years from people who thought the same as you. Didn't stop them getting a bloody good hiding though."

Martin dabbed the last of his gel over his brow.

"You sound like Bernie Grant now. I'll be fine Mum, and if I'm out all night, I'll give you a bell. I promise."

He slung on a shiny suede jacket and gave his mother a hug and a peck on the cheek.

"You just be careful of those two all right. I don't want you coming in off your head."

"It ain't going to happen, Mum."

He wondered if they'd changed much over the four years since he had seen his friends last. Two men rose in suits gleaming like they'd been painted with a light dusting of chrome.

"Bloody hell Mart, look at you. Good to see you mate. You been on the roids or something?"

Martin embraced his old friend.

"And you Joey, no mate, this is from graft. All right, George?"

George raised his corpulent frame from his stool and delivered a bear hug.

"Fine mate."

"Fine except he's been eating all the pies. Greedy fat sop he is now Mart, not like you I see. Those muscles for real or what?"

Martin bent his elbow and pointed at his biceps.

"Have a feel for yourself Joey. That's what two years of humping boxes about does for you."

"George, looks like you need to get a job at Martin's firm, mate."

George replied with a two fingered salute.

"There ain't nothing wrong with me. Jill loves a bit of blubber anyway."

Martin wondered what Mr. Yorke' would d make of his old drinking buddy.

"No chance, Joey. He'd have to work for his pay there."

"Make you right, mate. What you having?"

"Pint of Fosters for me."

Joey wiped the side of his empty glass, licking the last remnants of the taste of the west country..

"You drinking that Aussie pisswater. Have some Newquay Steam, it's the bollocks."

George nodded. Martin thought he might have graduated from the obedient poodle.

"Steam? Don't sound much like a drink to me."

Joey laughed and tilted his head back.

"Hi babes. Can you get my mate here a bottle of Steam and two more on top of that."

A hard-nosed shrew reached down to the fridge beneath the till.

"Babes? I'm old enough to be your mother and why don't you just ask for three bottles? I ain't half glad you don't do my premiums."

Joey passed over a tenner.

"I'd give you a good discount, Jane."

Change slammed down onto the bar. The barmaid sprung open the till, her attention already taken by the off duty security guard.

"You sell insurance then, Joey?"

"Yeah mate. I've just been promoted to client manager, it's easy money ripping off these boring sops with too much dosh in their hands."

Martin wrinkled his nose.

"I tell you what mate, you want to get yourself on my payroll. Loads to be made, mate. All you need is a bit of flannel."

Joey reached into his top pocket and flashed a wad of money at his old friend.

"Mate, you sure you want to be flashing that around in here?"

Martin looked over his shoulder. The patrons knocked back one pint after another and leapt into hilarity over a pair of trousers being yanked down.

"You're having a laugh ain't you? The punters in here are just like me, young, flash and flush. Besides, it was only a monkey, hardly going to set the world on fire, is it?"

Martin shrank when he calculated how long it would take to earn such a sum.

"Come on mate, drink up will you. We've got to be going soon."

He blinked.

"I thought we were having a few Sherbets in here. I don't want a heavy session tonight, Joey."

Joey slapped his friend's bicep.

"Come off it mate. We ain't seen you for time and 'sides it's my shout, least I can do."

The amber disappeared from its glass. Joey straightened his jacket before tossing a cigarette into his mouth.

"There you go mate."

Martin shook his head.

"Not for me. I can't hack the stink of fags in the morning."

Joey passed a cigarette to George.

"Yeah, I bet the stink of Harry Monk up your arse is well moody."

Martin tapped his friend on the arm with his fist.

"Hilarious you are. Where we off to then?"

The trio breezed into Borough High Street. Joey twirled a set of keys.

"A party of course, soppy. I've got a mate down Rotherhithe who's loaded. Tarts, booze, the whole works."

Martin walked past a shiny red motor parked at a daft angle until Joey pulled him up sharp.

"You got a G.T.I.? You kidding me?"

Martin leapt into the passenger seat much to George's protests.

"Shut it, fatty. You need all that room in the back-seat for yourself." said Joey.

George complained about his legs being to cramped and fidgeted from side to side.

"You sure you should be driving Joey? I ain't being funny but you've had a few."

Joey switched on the ignition and pressed the accelerator several times revelling at the sweet sound.

"Martin, are you my Mum? Lighten up and enjoy."

The car flew from the kerb and caught the edge of a parked Escort when it joined the mainstream of traffic.

"You just clobbered that motor."

Joey laughed when the G.T.I moved ever swifter.

"So what. I reckon I done him a favour putting my paintwork on his old banger."

Martin flinched when they missed a traffic island by inches.

"Oi, put your seat belt on. I'm a careful driver but you never know what might happen."

George chuckled in obedience in the back. Martin contemplated closing his eyes. His old friend long graduated from a loose cannon into an atomic bomb.

The distance soon passed. Joey yanked the handbrake.

"Magic, right then son, time for a bit of fun. This is my bosses gaff; Perry Atkinson."

Martin struggled to shake off the image of a pair of lorry headlights beaming into their motor. Joey's reflexes dared God and won.

"He might be my boss but the man's a nutter. It's going to be a night to remember."

The small gang escaped the confines of the car and followed Joey into a gravel path. Martin heard crazed house music escaping from the open windows above.

"You reckon they'll be able to hear us then?"

"Will you stop worrying? Of course they will."

"All right, Frankie?"

A tall man with a mushroom haircut embraced Joey.

"Glad you could come, mate. My brother is upstairs."

Frankie nodded when George said hello. His lip curled when his vision alighted on Martin.

"Who's that? I thought you were bringing a tart or two."

"I was going to mate, but they let me down."

Perry's sibling acted as the perfect human barricade.

"That explain him, does it?"

Martin inspected the pavement with unease clawing at his neck.

"Easy mate, you're being a bit unfriendly, ain't you? This is my friend who me and George used to hang around with. He's a laugh, salt of the Earth and he'll be sweet."

Frankie eased his head back.

"Go on then, but he better not misbehave."

Joey laughed.

"He bloody well better, Frankie."

The snarl surrendered into a smile. The three entered Perry's place. Two almost naked damsels curtsied and renewed kissing as they passed.

"What a shame eh, Mart? A shortage of tarts and those two have to be dykes."

One woman offered her middle finger to Joey before turning her attention back to her enthralled captive.

Martin gaped, his guide urged him to follow.

"Come on, we're off upstairs and we'll find Perry. You ain't seen nothing yet."

The three men passed several couples kissing and fondling on the stairs and landing. Joey paused at a set of large white painted double doors.

"Get ready to party."

The hedonistic gateway parted. The dance floor writhed with a host of pleasure seekers. Many were semi-clothed or naked and spun in dances of delirium. They groped, caressed or copulated to the sounds of feverish dance music whilst strobe lights flashed over their bodies. Martin walked in a realm of greedy fantasy. Several wild eyed figures enticed them to join in. Martin's attention leapt to a man in a velvet purple robe who sported a silver cane. He bowed and strode towards them.

"Good evening gentlemen. I'm so glad you've come to my small gathering."

Joey laughed before hugging the bizarre figure.

"Perry, this is mental mate."

The man nodded.

"Well, drop your strides and I'll see if I can get you in the mood."

"Piss off, you know I ain't ginger. You got anything for us? I want us to get in the mood."

Perry responded with a prurient grin.

"Why but of course. Here, please take with my pleasure and do feel free to use the bathroom."

Joey received a small plastic bag filled with red pills. He urged his cortège to follow.

"Nice one, boss. You're a legend."

Perry allowed his appraising eye to linger over Joey's new friend. He wondered what treasures lay beneath his fine trousers.

"I do believe I am. Listen young man, I'd be glad to take you somewhere a bit quieter if this gets a bit too much for you."

Martin whitened under the host's inspection.

"He ain't that way inclined, Perry. One hundred percent straight I'm afraid."

The man shook his head.

"What a shame, what a shame. Still, if you should change your mind dear, you only have to call."

Joey pushed his friend towards the bathroom.

"You didn't tell me he was gay."

"You didn't ask. He swings both ways and it's normally the birds he shags, but he might make an exception for you, gorgeous."

George performed his obedient chimp routine. His obsequious manner needled Martin.

"Sod off, Joey. What's in the bags?"

"Where have you been for the last four years, under a rock? This shit will take us to Orion and beyond."

The bathroom door yielded. Joey urged his friends to wait whilst he induced a chemical reaction. George took his turn and Joey passed the small bag of four pills to Martin.

"I dare you to go for three. Go on, the buzz is unreal."

Martin hadn't taken the chemical dance for over four years. His spirit protested when he picked up a small plastic tumbler from the side of the sink. His furtive hands opened the small plastic bag and he reached down to find narcotic treasure. The small red pills in his hand had the word S.E.X. emblazoned upon their carapace. He opened his mouth and placed all three tablets within before gulping down the contents of the glass in his hand. He closed his eyes and waited for revelation.

"Oi hurry up, Mart. You're holding us up out here," ordered Joey.

Martin looked towards the rattling door.

"No problems mate, just coming."

Martin blinked. He sensed a bizarre movement from the periphery of his left eye. He swivelled and once again the same experience grabbed him again. He clutched his stomach and nuclear butterflies raged within.

"Come on mate, let's get out there."

The door shook harder. Martin staggered to the entrance but stopped when a dark voice spat in triumph.

"You just fucked up, Marty. You've fucked up big style."

The door stood a foot away yet seemed an interminable distance from his outstretched left hand.

"You ready to dance, are you? That's good, because we'll see you on the floor, we can't wait."

Martin's head glittered in sweat, he burst outside looking for his friends eager to banish the invader.

"Martin, your friends are waiting. You don't want to let them down, do you?"

He groped for the handle and blinked when the swinging lights outside illuminated his eyes with a sense of destruction.

"About time. What was you doing in there?"

Martin grasped the side of his head seeking the elusive quality of balance.

"Nothing mate, just feel a bit weird. Just fuck off because something's off."

Joey recoiled when he caught the feral snarl on Martin's lips.

"Fucking all right ain't it? I haven't seen you for years, get you to the best night out in decades, sort out some free tabs for you and all you can do is tell me to fuck off?"

"I'm sorry mate but I'm feeling well odd. It must be the pills"

Joey's indignation disappeared as he spoke. Martin failed to hear. His vision fell on the dance floor where Perry presented a tray of canapés to his guests. His mind spun when Perry's robe shimmered before moving to a crazy beat of its own. The garment swelled into a solid black mass of liquorice metal.

Martin backed towards his friends who remained still as if in a temporal stasis. Martin glanced again at the rippled phantom robe. The darkness parted and the drug fuelled victim gasped when the robe spoke.

"Martin, I thought that was you over there. I see Joey and George are keeping you in mischief."

The robe floated across the dance floor and presented Martin a silver tray.

"You must enjoy the fruits of my dear partner's cooking. She's gone to a hell of a lot of effort. A hell of a lot."

Martin's forehead dripped in a spiral of incoherence. The sweat sprinted down his body and formed a silver pool of endless depth. He examined the contents of the robe's tray and flinched when the contents moved. He beheld many shapes which reminded him of chocolate bourbons, shortbreads, cookies and any other biscuit he could think of.

"Go on have one, they don't bite."

Martin's muscles stayed rigid whilst the tray danced close. The biscuits rose of their own accord. Martin discerned the slow evolution of cookie limbs and mouths on satanic chocolate. Their shadowy jaws opened and revealed jagged fangs eager to feast on ripe flesh.

"All right, I lied. They do bite a bit and they do like to nip."

The robe set the tray onto the floor. The biscuits decamped onto the dance arena. Their forms swelled to the height of around three feet and each one of the assortment sported something metallic in their left hand. Martin groaned when one of the cookies swung a butcher's cleaver from left to right.

"Feast my darlings, oh do indulge yourselves."

The sugar coated assassins snarled and their little legs sped into aggressive action. Martin lurched across the floor. The crazed beasts were quicker.

He urged his legs to find the exit yet the crazed confectionery headed him off. He threw his body towards the stairwell but met a solid wall of chocolate.

Martin pushed himself upright amidst a circle of the chattering hunters. He pleaded with the creatures but no words escaped his mouth. The biscuits swung their blades back and forth. Martin wondered why they never attacked. He looked around to see what they were waiting for. A solitary shadow fiend watched from outside the circle before calling several of its colleagues over to the night's entertainment.

"Hello Martin. Glad to see you again. You enjoying your little trip?"

The shadow nodded and the cookies attacked. He screamed when savage metal bit into his calf. The biscuits hacked into Martin and set about savage evisceration. Martin ribcage darted open to an inquisitive bourbon who snapped teeth onto a crimson bone. Another biscuit swung a meat cleaver into his neck and parted head from body.

The eyes in the victim's skull blinked when they shoved the head upon a pink wafer stave dripping in blood. His body rearranged like some reverse game of Operation. The biscuits grabbed his heart and indulged in a macabre game of basketball. A Jaffa Cake nibbled upon his sex and Martin waited for death. A presence hoisted his confused head by its hair and turned his face around. Martin looked into a solid shadow whose ethereal mouth parted as it prepared to feast. Martin screamed.

"What the matter with him," a dismembered voice yelled. Martin guessed it was Joey's.

"Your mate's lost it. He's off his head."

Several forms poked and prodded at the wriggling mass on their floor.

"Is he coming round? Is he going to be all right?" asked a girl from accounts.

Martin's body dragged itself upright. His eyes wide and glazed.

"Martin, can you hear me? You all right mate?"

The figure groped for his throat. Martin sighed, his neck remained intact yet a feeling of total nausea surged through his limbs and soul.

"No," croaked Martin.

"Get that prick out of here. You've got some explaining to do on Monday, Joey."

Martin gaped with bleary eyes at Perry. A red stream oozed down Perry's closed fist next to his nose.

"It's all right Perry, he just flipped mate. He didn't mean to punch you."

Martin looked to his bruised hand. His knuckles covered in blood.

"I don't know what happened. I was being attacked by something."

Perry shook his head.

"I don't give a toss. Fuck off and take your two mates with you and your biscuits or whatever the fuck you were raving about."

Martin struggled to his feet. Joey and George bore him away from a furious director.

"I'll sort it out, Perry. He just had a bad trip, that's all."

Martin's feet obeyed the slow beat of his heart whilst his friends led him away.

"Let's get you out of here."

Several faces stared at the embarrassed trio, some amused and more bemused.

"You've made things well dodgy for me mate. I ain't ever seen Perry as mad as that, not even when we lost one of our big accounts to Heath Investments. What did you have to hit him for?" Martin had no memory of breaking Perry's nose. His memory of being torn about by biscuits remained raw. His mind reeled and the world darkened.

They burst into night light. Martin broke away from Joey's grasp, eager for normality, eager never to see Joey and George ever again.

Chapter 17 Twinflame

Starlight flickered and grew in great streams of elemental flow into the waterfall of a life almost spent. Martin reached out dived across time and space. His despairing spirit urged him to stay; better to linger in the black hole of torment than risk the gift of rebirth. Martin's mind shrank back from fried memories of demonic biscuits and brutal dismemberment. The light intensified and the outline of an almost forgotten figure waved him forward.

"Come on son, don't give up."

Her voice a fire escape from the cruel citadel crushing his fight. The shades released their victim from bitter slumber. Her speech banished them to the spectral world of endless black. Martin glanced in wonder at his Lady Nel.

"Quick take my hand, come to your Nan," she pleaded.

Her voice strident. He fought through an endless fog to catch sight of her. He tried to stir yet chains of torment bit deep. His grandmother descended towards him.

"My beautiful child, hold out your hand."

His blurry eyes stared up to find her urging him to ascend. He urged his body to move, balancing on the threshold of darkness and salvation.

"Keep out your hand, my boy, keep it out now," ordered Nel.

Martin's strength diminished each moment. The shades edged back to the periphery of his spirit.

"Forget her, Martin. Forget your pointless life and come with us. There's nothing for you there."

The shade spoke with perfect reason. He looked to the abyss and welcomed the elixir of oblivion. To be forgotten, to be destroyed and to never have been. The dark thoughts lured him like those sweet pills of oblivion. He took a step back.

"Yes, come to us. Come away from her and those who give you nothing."

Martin's eye's sealed. Darkness enveloped him.

"Never, you let him go, foul creature," screamed Lady Nel. She grabbed Martin's wrist.

The shades fled from the woman's light. Martin almost choked when Nel allowed her strength to merge with her grandson's spirit. He soared with his grandmother, followed her to the sun as though she were an angelic Icarus. When Martin focused on Nel, he did not see a tired grey haired woman who sat at the end of his bed. Instead, a strong warrior who would dive into hell itself to save her family. Her love, warmth and power overwhelmed him.

"What a mess you've gotten yourself into. Look at you, you're all broken."

Martin blushed.

"Don't you get all downcast on me. I'm here to fix you."

Martin followed the lead of Nel's index finger. She pointed to the sun of life.

"Nan, won't we burn? I don't want to die."

Nel laughed.

"Die, oh you silly little boy. I'm going to make sure you live."

The flight's path quickened. Martin's skin screamed into awareness, his very soul protested at the magnetism of the sun. Martin shielded his eyes from incineration.

"Keep going Martin, we'll meet again soon enough, but not yet. Not yet."

"Nan, don't leave me. Don't leave me."

Flames breathed divine light upon him and the rapture of life ensnared him. He looked through the sun.

He witnessed a young man lying upon a bed flanked by two energies wrapped in a grey hue. A doctor thumped the chest of the dying man and shook his head. A sister and brother hugged and she screamed "Why?"

The man urged for a nurse to usher the grief stricken parent away. The doctor shook his head at the waste of another young life for a moment's chemical gold.

Martin escaped the sun and burst back into his shattered body. His spark illuminated the dead husk and dragged it to existence.

"I want to stay with him, please, I beg you," moaned his mother.

"I'm sorry Mrs. Lowe, I have to ask you to leave. There's nothing more we can do."

Martin's heart beat with new vigour. His body accepted the rush of air and ordered his lungs to function once again. He heard something fragile dropped by an astonished nurse. She pointed at the monitor betraying the ghost of new life.

"Mum," gasped Martin.

She seized his hand in a firm grip. Her utter distress transformed to the butterfly of hope.

"That's impossible. He was dead, he had to be."

Rose turned to the Doctor.

"Not impossible Doctor, it's a miracle."

Rose hugged her reborn offspring, much to the astonishment of the Doctor.

"That's not a good idea Mrs. Lowe. We really should be very careful about Martin."

"Oh bollocks. He's my Son and I almost lost him."

Her love poured into him and she held him close through a raw red misty veil.

"Mrs. Lowe, I must insist."

The doctor persuaded Rose to loosen her grip.

"Come on, follow Nurse Wright and she'll make you a cup of tea. We've all had a massive shock to say the least."

Martin pointed to the exit whilst his mother remained.

"Go on Mum, I'll be fine. Honest."

She followed her guide and the doctor narrowed his eyes in judgement.

"Young man, you don't need me to tell me how lucky you've been. The amount of drugs you pumped into your body was plain crazy, crazy."

Martin's stomach spat fury as if to sympathise with the Doctor's words.

"I know, Doc. Things got out of hand. I'm sorry."

"You shouldn't be apologising to me, Martin. For all intents and purposes, you should be dead."

Martin winced at the memory of diabolical confectionery.

"Yes, I was elsewhere Doc, and I came back. I came back and this is never going to happen again."

"That's enough of a lecture for me for now. Rest assured young man, I'll have plenty more to say on the matter when you're better."

Martin agreed. His eyes loaded with iron, rolled down.

"I'll leave you to rest. You look like you've been to hell and back. I'll see that your Mum…"

He never heard the rest of the sentence. He needed to sleep, sleep a long while.

"You looking forward to going back to work soon then?"

"I just want to get back to normal, Mum."

Martin, for the first time in his life, couldn't wait for Monday. It was three weeks since the incident and watching the daily intake of banal Australian adventures drove him to insanity.

"Glad to hear it. Listen, can you do us a favour?"

"Sure."

His mother stuffed a ten pound note in his hand.

"Go down the road and get us a few bits and bobs. I've got a list for you."

Martin almost preferred the soaps before taking his order.

"No problem. I'll see you in a while."

The fresh air stung his lungs. He squinted at the tiny writing on paper.

2 pints of milk

1 loaf - make sure it's brown

Big bag of ready salted crisps

40 B&H

1 bottle of ketchup

Martin gave up reading the rest and stuffed the note into his pocket. He shuffled along and shuddered when a hand tapped him on his shoulder. He spun with his hand tightening into a fist: there was no way he was going to be mugged for a tenner. The upsurge in aggression dissipated when the angel of his regret appeared before him.

"All right, Mart?"

Stacey. He wanted to see her for so long, to put things right. She stood before him in the middle of a Saturday morning with bags of uncertainty swimming behind nervous eyes.

His mind clouded in a sea of delirium. There were so many things he wanted to say.

"What's the matter? Cat got your tongue or something?"

She giggled and he reciprocated.

"Stacey, God, it's good to see you again."

She remained the same girl he knew, only older and the vestiges of womanhood won the battle over the naive adolescent he knew. She was more than beautiful; she was his partner. The ghost of his stupidity howled deep within.

"Yeah, great to see you again, Martin. It's been a long time."

"Too long. I was such a fool, Stace."

She sentenced him to silence with a finger on his lips. He stared deep into her azure eyes and their mouths joined in a celebratory reconnection.

They paused enraptured by the sorcery of an unexpected reunion. Stacey reached behind Martin's head and grasped a clump of his blonde hair and dragged him close as she inhaled him back into her life.

"Wow, Stace."

Her small hand found its way into his own. Martin grasped it firm but not so hard as to cause her discomfort.

"I've missed you so much, Mart."

"Stacey, how could I have ever let you go?"

She laughed, tossed her head back, sending waves through her raven mane.

"We were so young, Mart. Too young I suppose, but we had something."

"Something special, Stace."

Martin eased his hands around her shoulders and drew her even tighter.

"I was a dumb kid, Stacey."

The pair kissed again and a tacit pact of divine love passed between them.

"What happens now then, Mart?"

His gentle fingers caressed her ears before stroking the side of her face.

"Now? How about we find somewhere quiet and you know?"

Stacey leaned in closer, smelt the fragrance of Right Guard.

"You always knew how to impress a girl," she laughed,"still, got to admit it sounds good to me."

He hardened when she pressed. He looked to the outline of a hideaway beyond the high street.

"How about the park? There's a row of bushes at the back."

"Piss off. I'm not getting all mucked up in the bushes, even for you. I'm a woman now, not a soppy little girl. Come on, let's go for a walk," instructed Stacey.

"I'm sorry Stace, but I'm struggling to think of a good spot. We could find an hotel but I'm broke."

She leaned her head onto his shoulders.

"It's OK, I've got an idea."

Martin, hopped in impatience. Stacey put her fingers on her lips.

"You'll have to wait and see. Anyway, haven't you got some things to get?"

"Yeah, how'd you know?"

"Bloody hell Mart, I think the name of the shop kind of gives it away."

He never realised they arrived at the supermarket so fast.

"Yeah, Mum asked me to get a few bits and bobs and then I have to get back. I'm half-tempted to throw the list away and find out your little secret."

"You'll do nothing of the sort. Come on, let's shop together and we can say hi to your Mum."

Rose grew impatient when the hour strolled by.

"I'll kill him when he gets home. He only had a few things to get."

Danny took little heed of his mother's bluster.

"He'll be all right, Mum. He's probably run into a mate or something."

"Oh one of his ex-junkie mates no doubt. Probably try and get him back in that bloody hospital again."

Danny regretted his words when Rose approached the door.

"What you doing, Mum?"

"What'd you think I'm doing? I'm going to look for him of course. I'll not have those tossers ruin his life again."

"Mum," protested her youngest son. "Sit down and relax, he's not sixteen anymore."

Danny ushered his mother back to her chair and eased the coat from her back.

"If something's happened to him I'll never forgive myself, Dan. Never."

Danny exhaled when the door swung inward.

"About bloody time," she exploded, "Where'd you go? Bloody China?"

Martin laid the bag of groceries onto the kitchen worktop.

"Sorry Mum, I bumped into an old friend, that's all."

Rose's heart sank. She thought her son was finished with 'that' life.

"Oh Martin, you promised me. You said you'd never speak to them again."

He nodded.

"I did and I mean not to speak to them, Mum. They're a bunch of losers. Anyway, I reckon you'll like my new old friend. You used to get on pretty well, if I remember."

Danny and his mother were baffled by Martin's words. Rose prayed he didn't dance in some strange hallucination.

"Really? All right Mart, why don't you tell me who it is then and we'll have a good talk about it."

"I'll do better than that Mum. I'll introduce my friend to you."

Martin walked back into the hallway and Rose prepared for a meeting with the invisible man.

"Mum, meet Stacey."

The pair kissed on the threshold. Rose's fears vanished into pure bliss. She hated Martin when he dismissed her for self destruction.

"Hi Mrs. Lowe, good to see you again."

The matriarch of the flat laughed.

"Oi, it's Rose to you. Come here and give me a hug," she opened her arms and Stacey sped towards her, "and as for you and your teasing."

Martin flinched when his mother winked in his direction.

"What? I told you she was a friend, she's well, a bit special, that's all."

"I'll see you later, Martin Lowe. What'd you want to drink, Stace? Cup of tea or something a bit stronger. You'll have to tell me about your mother. Is she all right? Do you still live at the same place? Are you at work? Are you all right?"

"Easy Mum. She came up to see us all not to get the third degree."

Rose's cheeks reddened.

"Oh, don't mind me love. It's just so good to see you again after all these years. Whatever happens between you and dopey over there, don't ever be a stranger again."

Stacey sipped from a steaming fresh cup of PG.

"I'll stay in touch Rose, I promise. Somehow though, I think you'll be seeing a lot more of me."

Martin joined his mother in embarrassment when Stacey stared straight at him. She never judged when Martin recalled the errors of his life when they walked back to the flat from the supermarket. He loved her strength of forgiveness as well as her beauty. He unburdened his pain onto her small shoulders and she bore the weight with little hint of sadness.

She winced when he explained the despair that claimed him when he told her of the death of their old friend. He revealed how it tore him apart. She soothed him when he spoke of his descent into drugs and benefit dependence and embraced him when he found pride at last in his job. She paled at the recent revelation of his last dealings with his old friends and how it almost claimed his life. He promised he was himself again and how he loved her all those years ago.

"That's the best news I've had all year, Stace. That boy needs someone in his life and I'm just glad you're around."

"Sounds like he's been a right pain in the arse, Rose."

"You don't know the half of it. I tell you there were times I could have swung for him."

"I can imagine."

Martin stared with his mouth agape.

"Oi, I am here, you know."

Rose had a good feeling about Stacey and her son, a deep connection that could not be moved. Stacey intended to stay for half an hour. The day disappeared into ghosts of discussion and the hour of midnight called and vanished.

"I've got to go, Mart. God's it good to see you again."

Martin moved closer to his old soulmate.

"You don't have to go, Stace. You can stay if you like."

Her eyes scrunched up and her lips pursed in dilemma.

"Oh Mart, I don't know. What about your Mum, won't she mind?"

She glanced to the staircase where Rose had retired an hour before.

"Mind? No, she'll be as good as gold trust me."

"Sounds like you've done this before then."

Stacey looked down to her feet. Martin grasped her hands and stared into her hurt eyes.

"Not for ages, Stace. Only when I was stupid."

She rewarded him with a light peck on his cheek.

"So what, you're old and wise then now, are you?"

"Don't know about that," he snorted. "Just a bit older and loved up, I reckon."

"What you saying, Mart?"

Martin slid his hands around his girlfriend's hips.

"What I'm saying Miss Wells, is I've been the biggest fool that ever lived. What I'm saying, Miss Wells, is I want us to be together from now on. What I'm saying is I love you Stacey, always have."

He looked into her eyes and recognition within burst into life.

"I love you too, Mart."

Their lips joined and the two melted into each other. The memory of old teenage connection vanishing into a creation of profound gravitas.

"Let's go to bed," urged Martin.

Stacey nodded.

"I will. I've got to call Mum first though."

"Course. You get on the blower and I'll sort things out upstairs. See you soon."

Martin's mind raced. He envisioned the future when the pair set up home together. He visualised their children and Stacey becoming Mrs. Lowe. He once would have laughed off such thoughts as sad, yet now he set out to craft their own beautiful path.

He stripped off and stood by the door and gasped when Stacey walked in having already loosened her blouse and bra. They kissed hard, in the deepest yearning either imagined and settled into bed, slaves to passion and soulmates joined together and unbreakable in union.

Chapter 18 Together forever

Martin gazed at the promise of independence. His frame coasted into the unusual position of steering and his solar plexus sung with the touch of a hundred woodpeckers enquiring at this foolish step.

"You reckon they're doing it for the state of your health, do you? Trust me, a year of driving and dropping will soon piss you off. Do yourself a favour and just remain a driver's mate."

He dismissed his uncle's unease. They were a good team. He took Stacey for a long walk the previous evening and looked at several places with the temptation of 'for sale' outside.

"I know. Still, at least I'll have a bit more cash in the old sky rocket."

Jim shook his head in resignation.

"Dare say that young tart of yours will spend it for you."

"Oi, she ain't no tart, you miserable old git," snapped Martin.

Martin learned the value of rediscovering his soul mate over the last few weeks. Stacey's presence victorious over the ghosts of vice and annihilation.

"All right, don't bite my bloody head off. All I'm saying is be a bit careful."

The lorry pulled up and Martin's animus departed.

"You worry too much, Jim. I know exactly what I'm doing and trust me, so does Stace."

His uncle scowled a farewell whilst Martin fumbled with his house keys as his Mum opened the door.

"Mum, Something up?" He thought it strange to see Rose waiting for him.

"I dunno. Stacey's inside and says she needs to talk to you. Is there something you need to tell me?"

Martin shook his head and brushed his mother aside. Stacey stood and they exchanged a kiss, much to the embarrassment of his brother.

"Cut it out will you."

"No chance."

Stacey nudged her boyfriend in the stomach.

"Oi, don't be nasty, Mr. Lowe." said Rose.

"Stace, what's this about you wanting to see me about something?"

His girlfriend found the crumpled remains of the morning paper more comfortable to view that Martin's curious gaze.

"What is it? You've got me worried now."

Rose went to the kitchen on the pretence of making a cup of tea. She asked his brother to him to help her make some sandwiches, much to his annoyance.

"We need to talk, Martin. Something's happened and I'm scared."

Stacey cast her eyes to the stairs.

"Shall we go to my office then?"

Her small hand nestled inside his own and she led the way before hovering at the end of her lover's bed. Martin sat on the mattress and beckoned for Stacey to do likewise.

"It's all right, I think I'll stand."

She inhaled. Martin's thoughts battled wasps of worry. He clenched his fists at the thought of a terrible betrayal or a dreadful illness.

"What's going on? Just tell me."

"All right, this ain't easy Mart. It's bloody hard."

"Just get it off your chest, Stace. You can tell me anything, you know that."

His words trickled through her shield of dread like daggers of comfort.

"Martin, I'm pregnant."

He swallowed hard, disbelief his new master. The precautions they took ensured their passions restricted them to two souls in love.

"The twenty first, Mart. It must have been then."

His throat roared in dry fire.

"Martin, say something. I'm so sorry."

He left the bed and stood face to face, a bubbling feeling swirling ever upwards to his heart and to her terrified face.

"Darling, you've got nothing to say sorry about. Especially as this is the best news I've ever heard in my life."

Stacey's heart jumped when Martin placed his hand on her belly.

"You're not angry then? I thought you'd go mad."

"Mad? You're mad for thinking that girl. Come here, both of you."

Martin kissed her and her fears evaporated in his paternal embrace. He swayed in delirium and the dreams of days, months, years and decades dominated his young mind.

"We're going to have to sort a few things out, Stace. For one, I ain't going to bring up a bastard and we'll have to sort a place out."

Stacey's mind belly-flopped in realisation.

"Are you proposing? You mean, you want us to get married?"

"What, don't you want to be called Stacey Lowe then? Something wrong with my name?"

She brushed her hair back as the smell of tuna escaped from Rose's kitchen.

"Of course not, silly."

Martin pulled Stacey's ear close to his lips and whispered.

"Stacey Wells, will you marry me?"

She spat the answer in a heartbeat.

"With all my heart yes. God, I love you."

"I love you too, darling. Come on, let's go downstairs and give Mum a heart attack."

The two embraced as they kissed again and again relishing the gift of creation. Martin struggled to comprehend how his life changed so much in the last six months. His thoughts turned to new life and their joint freedom.

They found Rose standing with arms folded across her chest. His brother tried to look disinterested in the cage of a paper.

"Mum, Daniel, me and Stacey have got a bit of an announcement."

Danny straightened up at the sound his full Christian name. He swore Martin never used it before.

"What is it? We're all on tenterhooks here." said Rose.

Martin's sweaty brow betrayed his attempts at calmness. Stacey tucked her hand into his and he took her strength as his own.

"Me and Stacey, well, we've decided to get married."

Danny sighed whilst Rose released a huge smile. She raced forward, eager to embrace them both.

"Oh that's wonderful Martin. It really is."

Martin held his hands outstretched to ward her off.

"There's more, Mum. Stacey's pregnant and we're going to get ourselves a place together."

"Bloody hell Mart, you don't mess about, do you mate?" said Danny.

The couple braced themselves for an outburst yet Rose's happiness leapt to the height of the Nat West Tower.

"You mean I'm going to be a grandmother?"

She restrained herself no more. She remembered the days when her son cried at the foot of his bed when their father left, she remembered the days when his best friend died, she recalled the days when he stared at the edge of the abyss and dared to try to fight back at life. She remembered his encounter with death and the ever growing maturity shining forth. The thought of her little boy making the transformation to man, husband and father urged her to embrace him and his wife-to-be.

"Oh Martin, I'm so proud of you. Aren't you, Danny?"

Danny scanned the results from the night before in the Sun.

"Yeah great. Does that mean I get his room then? Does that mean I'm going to be an uncle to Martin's sprog?"

Stacey shot him a vicious glare.

"Danny, a little bit of joy wouldn't go amiss, you miserable sod." said Martin.

Rose waved her youngest son's lack of enthusiasm away.

"Oh don't worry about him. He's been a right old sourpuss lately. Now, what are you going to do about getting a place then?"

Martin glanced at the South London Press.

"Start looking in there I suppose and try and find somewhere. We'll stick ourselves on the council list as well."

"You want to get cracking on that score straight away. I'll have a word with Charlie downstairs, he knows a couple of people who might be able to pull a few strings for you."

Stacey nodded.

"Thanks Rose, that's really nice of you."

Rose dismissed the appreciation.

"Don't mention it love. You'll be calling me Mum soon and talking of which, you told your parents yet?"

The pair shook their heads.

"Well, you better get round there and tell them."

Martin dreaded the upcoming meeting. Mr and Mrs Wells never did like him much, especially her father.

"Yes we better, Mart. Shall we go now?"

He looked for an excuse but his mother's finger pointed him in the direction of the door.

"No time like the present. Go on, you've told me, so I'm sure you can tell Stace's mum and dad."

"Don't worry love, leave the talking to me. It'll be fine." assured Stacey.

Martin adapted to a new brother called exhaustion. Overtime upon never ending days merged into weeks of eternal labour. He trudged up the stairwell, ignoring two drunken men arguing before the larger of the two punched his drinking partner, knocking him to the floor. He sidestepped the fallen sot before carrying on to the flat and prayed for a day of peace and rest.

"All right love, I'm home."

A cheerful reply came from the kitchen told him dinner was ready. Stacey emerged from the doorway and Martin adored her standing larger than ever with their unborn child.

"I can't wait to get somewhere better than this shithole, Stace. I just dodged two pissheads having a row."

"I wondered what all the racket was out there."

Martin pulled his fiancée close and their lips pressed together.

"So how's my young lady then? Taking care of my little one, is she?"

Stacey pulled away. Martin sought her lips once again.

"Oi, less of the young lady, cheeky. And it's our little one." she added before she yielded to amorous intentions. Martin slid his hand inside her blouse.

"Ain't you gonna have dinner first?" she yelped when his other hand eased its way inside her trousers.

"I'm having dinner right now. I've had a dreadful day and the only thing that's kept me going is the thought of you and your tits. They're fucking huge."

Stacey gasped when Martin clawed her clothes off.

"Well, you better make the most of it. Especially with baby getting ever bigger, that's who my tits will be for, not you."

Martin kissed her again before finding his way inside.

"Never mind baby getting bigger, it's me who's getting bigger now."

"Can't say I noticed," teased Stacey.

The lovers removed their clothing, merged in gentle adoration. Stacey appreciated her partner's gentleness before he found his release.

"Come on, get dressed and let's have some grub. I've done a nice casserole tonight."

The two retired to the kitchen. Martin's vacant stomach relished a well-earned feast.

"That was class, Stace. Best meal you've done yet I reckon."

She trusted her lover spoke the truth.

"Better than your Mum's?"

She thought the question would cause him a problem yet Martin surprised her.

"Easily, Mum does good grub but yours is great, darling. Maybe a bit too good."

He tapped his stomach to emphasise the point.

"You'll get smaller portions then. There's only one of us round here who's pregnant."

He shook his head.

"Don't you dare woman. I'll soon whip myself into shape down the gym, won't I?"

Stacey stared with lascivious eyes.

"You don't necessarily have to go the gym, love. There's other ways."

"Don't you want to do the washing up first?"

Stacey opened her blouse and exposed her breasts once again. Martin reached out towards her.

They cleared the table and Stacey reclined and him invited him forward.

"Time for afters then?"

"You better believe it, lover boy. Plenty of time for afters. Love you."

Martin kissed her again.

"Love you too, darling."

Chapter 19 A New Gift

Martin thought the clouds hid a few sharks for the rain rolled down in endless waves. He grabbed the door of Ossie's Plaice and welcomed the heat and smell of fish and fat.

"Marty, good to see you mate. What'll it be?"

He brushed away rivulets of water from his brow before they turned to sweat.

"Two cod, a couple of portions of chips and a saveloy. Splash on loads of that onion juice. Can't go wrong with that squire."

The balding black-haired cook nodded.

"Too right. My family swear by it, reckons it stops you losing your hair."

Martin gave him a puzzled look before bursting out in laughter.

"You wally, you almost had me there."

Ossie's façade of seriousness wavered.

"It was a good story though. Onion juice on chips, it's my idea of heaven."

The shop filled with the sound of the batter creation. Ossie plunged the cod in and whistled.

"I'll give you the best two pieces of cod I have and extra chips too."

"Cheers mate, you're a star."

Martin inhaled the fatty scent and his stomach quivered in impatience. He skipped lunch to work through and the end of the shift seemed never to arrive.

"I bet you're both counting the days? I remember when my Timmy was born. I was so happy Martin, so proud."

"You must have been mate. How long ago was it?"

The Turk frowned for a moment in thought.

"Oh, must be seventeen years ago now. Little Tim isn't so little anymore. He's a proper pain in the arse. Still worth it though, he'll be a good man."

Martin glanced towards to the box in the corner to see Millwall go one up on the teletext.

"Oi, oi, one up against the scum. I tell you what Ossie, this is turning out to be one blinding day, even if God's taking a leak."

Ossie waved a finger.

"Hey, don't be disrespectful."

Ossie popped open several sheets of paper.

"I didn't take you as the religious type."

A hunk of fish smacked into wrapping.

"Not as a rule, but it ain't clever to go looking for trouble is it? I mean he's got enough things on his mind without you taking the piss out of him taking a piss, if you see what I mean."

Martin didn't but agreed anyway.

"There we go. All wrapped up and say hello to Stace for me won't you?"

"Thanks Chief, keep the change."

Ossie thanked Martin for his generosity before his customer dived back into the tempest.

Martin jogged back in the torrent praying the carrier bag shielded their meal from saturation. His key scrambled in the front door.

"Mart, is that you?"

"No, it's the Pope. Course it's me."

She didn't respond. Martin's humour surrendered to gravitas when she struggled through the living room doorway.

"You all right?"

The food nestled in an armchair. Martin ushered his wife towards the sofa.

"It's started, Mart. I think you better call an ambulance."

"What you mean, now?"

Stacey snarled yes. Martin punched in 999.

"He's on his way darling. Is there anything you need? Water, tea or even the fish and chips? Fucked if I know what."

He mopped her brow. Beads of sweat filled the towel. He thundered over to the window.

"Hope they don't take too long. You sure there's nothing I can do?"

Stacey shook her head.

"Yeah, stop worrying. I've enough on my plate without you going nuts as well."

Martin paced back and forth desperate for a glimpse of a van of deliverance.

"I'm going to ring Mum. She'll know what to do, probably be a lot more useful than a muppet like me."

He dialled her number. Stacey agreed to his common sense. His mum left the house in less than a minute.

"She'll meet us at the hospital, Stace. Where is that frigging ambulance?"

He tried to keep calm, to reassure, yet threatened to explode in impatience.

"Martin, for God's sake calm down. You'll make the baby come early if you carry on like that."

He sat, stood, sat, stood and sat again. Stacey prepared to protest when the doorbell rang.

"About time."

He allowed in two paramedics joking about the torrential rain before they strolled over to Stacey.

"All right Mrs. Lowe? Good. We'll have you off to hospital in no time at all. I take it you're coming, Mr. Lowe?"

The gentle interrogation continued. One of the pair escorted Martin to the kitchen.

"It'll be a just a little while before we're ready to go. Just got to sort a few things to sort out and we'll be on our way."

"She's not going to give birth in here, is she?" panicked the expectant father.

"No, no fear of that. Just a few women things that's all. Tell you what, me and Shirley haven't had a cuppa for ages now. Be a devil and make us one each, will you? No sugar in mine and one in Shirl's."

"You sure we got time?"

"Just about if you get to it."

Martin set to work with sugar and milk and dared the kettle to boil faster.

"Fuck's sake hurry up, will you."

"Beg your pardon?" said the paramedic.

"Nah, not you, this bloody kettle. Always takes ages."

The paramedic glided past Martin and pressed a small switch.

"Helps if you press the on button."

"How the bollocks did I miss that? Sorry about that."

"Don't worry about it, Martin. You'd be astonished at the amount of times that's happened. Guess there is a lot on your mind."

Hot water gushed into cups resplendent with teabags.

"You could say that. There you go."

"Almost ready, John." Said Shirley.

John declined the steaming cup.

"Thanks for the offer Martin, but baby wants to come now. We'd best be on our way."

Shirley helped Stacey down to the ambulance. Martin followed with barely a neighbour taking any notice. Stacey and himself hunted for comfort in the confines of the ambulance.

Despite the sirens, progress was slow. Hitting Denmark Hill at half past five wasn't the best of timing. A skirmish of nurses and doctors waited for Stacey and her entourage. Martin trailed his wife after the briefest of farewells and gratitude to the ambulance drivers.

"Try to relax Mrs. Lowe. Baby will soon be with us. Mr. Lowe, please stand back. That's it Stacey, nice big breaths. Remember to push when we say. Mr. Lowe, please stand to one side. That's it, onto the bed Stacey. Here, take some gas. Mr. Lowe, I must insist you stand to one side or I'll ask you to leave. No, if you want him to stay Stacey, I suppose we can let him. I know it hurts but you keep pushing, Stacey. That's fantastic. A real big effort now Stacey and baby will be with us."

Martin kissed his wife's fingers. He lost count of how many times he'd done that. He looked to the door and sighed with deep relief.

"There you are. I've been searching all over the hospital for you two."

Rose took residence on the opposing side of the bed.

"For God's sake Martin, ease up on Stacey's hand, will you?"

His guilty grip relented. An embarrassed father to be smiled an apology to his wife who despite the agony reciprocated.

"That's fantastic, Stacey. One more big effort and baby will be with us. Take some more gas and give it all you've got."

Rose swept her daughter-in-law's matted hair away from her brow. She dabbed her forehead with a convenient handkerchief.

"You're doing fantastic, a bit bleeding better than that idiot son of mine."

They giggled despite Martin's protestations.

Stacey squeezed with all her strength. Her womb stretched to thresholds of pain beyond endurance.

"I can see the head Mrs Lowe. We're almost there."

Stacey strayed beyond the veil of consciousness before letting her muscles contract and relax. Her vision reddened for the briefest of moments whilst lucidity swam with delirium. A beautiful sound dragged her from her swoon: the music of a baby crying. Her baby. Their baby.

"Congratulations, Mrs. Lowe. It's a beautiful baby girl."

A tiny figure snuggled within the arms of an adoring mother. Martin struggled to speak.

"I can't believe it, it's our baby," over and over. The team severed the umbilical cord and their baby found her voice once again.

"Oh, she's so beautiful Mart. We still going to call her Kelly then?"

Martin disappeared into the rapture of new life. Teeny fingers grasped hold of his index finger and in that moment the bond of father and daughter was forever sealed.

"Oh yeah babe. That's our Kelly all right and yeah, she's bloody gorgeous."

Kelly glanced around, terrified of her new surroundings. Fresh eyes scoured for guidance and discovered solace when they locked onto Rose.

"She's a special one. You two better look after her, or you'll have me to deal with. Make sure you do a damn better job of it than your flaming father ever did."

Martin looked at his newly completed family and agreed with every word his mother said.

"I'll do anything for her, Mum. Absolutely anything. She's the most wonderful thing that's ever happened to us."

Rose stared hard at her son with undeniable pride and happiness in her heart.

Kelly screamed, Stacey stroked her brow before holding her in a gentle embrace.

"She's so beautiful, ain't she Mart? So perfect."

"Goodnight babe."

The baby stared up from her cot and giggled when Martin turned his fingers into pretend aeroplanes. They had been home for three weeks and the link between his own little family staggered him. He worried at her tiny delicate form. His eyes scoured her bedroom for hidden dangers again and again.

"You coming to bed, love?"

Martin slid a wispy hair from Kelly's brow.

"Yep, just on my way, Stace."

His daughter laughed once more before the light faded. Martin had no idea he was so comical. He rubbed his eyes before glancing once more into her room. A gasp caught in his throat. An apparition of a woman stood at the foot of the cot, laughing and soothing her great granddaughter. Her dead eyes turned to Martin and he recalled the beautiful smile she used to offer him and her stories floated up from his buried memories. He didn't say a word but returned his grandmother's love, assured his daughter lived in a sanctuary of safety.

Chapter 20 A Proper Dad

"You going to have a word with her or is it down to Muggins again?"

Martin dreamt of an early night and settling down with his wife for a relaxing time watching the box. Two men had been off sick from Martin's shift. He'd had to stay two hours behind to help out.

"Stace, I've just got in. At least let me wind down a bit."

His wife slammed a cup onto the side.

"Wind down. Well mate, you can wind down whilst she winds me up. It's your fault undermining me all the bloody time."

"What are you on about, woman?"

Stacey's eyes flared.

"Your cow of a daughter, that's what. First, she comes in late from school. Second, she tells me it's none of my business and third, she's off swanning out yet again. That's the third time this week. I tell you Martin, I'm not going to be treated like shit anymore."

Kelly's father drained the remnants of a glass of water. He didn't treat himself to alcohol until Friday.

"All right, all right I'll have a word. Where is she now?"

"Don't you bloody listen? Out, O. U. T., out."

Martin glanced at his watch.

"It's gone half ten though."

"Tell me something I don't know. She's taking the piss."

Martin reached for his mobile and banged buttons.

"Sorry babe, for all this. I'll get it sorted."

Stacey folded her arms, scowled in impatience. She couldn't believe a fourteen-year old girl could cause such mayhem.

"Voice mail, for God's sake."

"What'd you expect? Anyway, I'll get your sodding dinner."

Martin wiped the ever increasing flow of sweat from his brow.

"Kelly, it's Dad. Call me straight away when you hear this and get your arse home."

Stacey hurled down a tray and a plate of chicken and chips onto a chair in front of the settee. Her daughter grunted a Mum, now and then and not much else. Martin got her best side, a smile, a laugh and she'd secure a score for her pocket every time.

"Don't say anything babe. I should have listened to you a bit more, no, a lot more but it's hard, you know."

"Hard? You should try living with the little bitch twenty-four seven. That's bloody hard, especially when Daddy gets his daughter everything she wants and can do no wrong."

"All right, I know she can wrap me round her little finger. Trust me though Stace, I'll sort it. Soon as she gets home, I promise."

Martin struggled with icy guilt. He glanced at the rings under his wife's eyes and cursed his own blindness.

"I wish you luck, that's all I can say. She'll probably tell you to piss off."

"You what? When has she ever said that to you?"

"About twenty times a week."

Martin pushed his dinner aside. He rose infuriated at another black spot in his knowledge.

"Why didn't you tell me? Bloody hell, Stace."

"What's the point? You won't do anything, will you?" screamed Stacey.

Her outburst heralded a ravine of tears. Martin allowed her to crumple under his embrace whilst his anger continued to rise.

"I'm so sorry, Stace. Babe, I promise you I won't let you feel like this again. No way."

The pair cuddled ever tighter and the living room door squeaked open.

"Mum, Dad, everything all right?"

A child of twelve wiped sleep from his young eyes. Stacey shied away from her son, her tears continued to rain on Martin's shoulders.

"Get back to bed, son. We'll be all right in a bit."

"You sure Dad? Where's Kel?"

Martin offered a fake smile and pointed to the bedroom.

"Yeah I'm sure, Ads. Your sister will be in later, go on get some kip, I don't want you up late for school."

A croaky OK followed. His son's voice breaking made Martin think he listened to a Aled Jones on steroids. He found no laughter tonight though. His thoughts veered to his tortured wife.

"Come on babe, sit down. I'll make you a cuppa."

She mumbled in assent. Martin guided Stacey to the settee, almost afraid to let her go.

"Thanks love. I'm sorry for going off on one, but Kelly, she's really getting to me."

"Oi, you don't need to apologise, Stace. And as for our young lady, her feet won't touch the ground when I get hold of her."

He planted a kiss on Stacey's brow. Her husband stormed into the kitchen. Stacey allowed herself a smile, at least her husband came to her side at last. Her thoughts were invaded by a fanfare of frantic dance music.

"Kelly, where the fuck are you?"

Martin gripped his phone so hard Stacey swore she thought he'd break it.

"Dad? What you on about?"

"You, what are you doing out at this time of night? You should be in your bed."

A heavy sigh responded.

"But Dad, I told Mum I was going round Tina's tonight. We're only listening to some tunes, it's not like we're having a piss up or anything."

"Get your arse home now. I'll not have my daughter roaming the streets of South London this time of night."

"But Dad, that's going to make me look sad. Besides, I could always crash out."

"Get home now, I ain't asking again." he roared.

Martin seldom exploded and Stacey, like her daughter, recoiled at the outburst.

"Dad that's just so unfair. I'll look like a ten-year old."

"I don't care if you look like a telly tubby. You just do as your told, go and get a cab."

"I ain't got any money though."

"Don't worry about that, I'll sort out the cab from this end."

His daughter sighed and snarled an address.

"Well I suggest you get ready, young lady. We're going to have a little chat, you and I."

"What about Mum then?"

Martin exhaled in exasperation.

"I think you've given your Mum enough grief for one day, don't you?"

Kelly protested. Her father ignored her pleas and ordered her home.

"Do you want to go to bed, love? I don't want you getting in the crossfire when Lady Muck gets home."

Stacey steeled herself to present a united front.

"Go on, go to bed, Stace. You've had enough for one day."

She yawned and Martin took her hand. She welcomed the wave of fatigue.

Martin wrapped his leathery arms around his wife, too tired to speak. She absorbed his strength, his shield of safety."

"I'm so sorry about all this, Stace. I just had no idea."

He cradled her head running his fingers through her hair. She looked into Martin's vibrant eyes and enjoyed the touch of the man she loved for so long.

"I love you, Stacey Lowe, don't you ever forget that."

They kissed. Martin took his wife to bed and allowed his hurricane to come to life.

At last the key wrestled with the lock. Martin stood up after his first born slammed the door behind her. He glared at a girl whose innocence decayed every day and shook his head in indignation. Her hair black and plaited and she painted far too much eyeliner on her face. She dyed her natural blonde locks and her lips pulsed with an abundance of lipstick.

An obsidian coloured dress swung too high above her knees for her Dad's liking and her midriff sported a fake chain-mail blouse. Her body reeked of cheap perfume along with the stench of nicotine.

"You been smoking?"

"What if I have? And what's with bringing me back so early? It's only half ten for God's sake."

Martin blew out his cheeks and curled his hands into fists. The sight of his daughter, haughty and offended standing in the passageway and her mother reduced to a helpless wreck broke the cap of rage.

"Right, I've just about had enough of your crap young lady. There you are dressed up like some cheap tart and going on about it being bloody early. Have you any idea what you're doing to your mother? Well? Have you?"

His daughter bristled at the ever increasing volume of her Dad's voice.

"It would have been fine if she would just let me get on with my life."

"Shut it. I'm talking, not you, it's not enough she has to look after the house without putting up with your shit. Anyway, if you think half ten's early, here's something else for you. You ain't going out the house for another week."

"Oh my God. You can't do that, it's out of order."

"Out of order? Tell you what, seeing as it's so out of order you ain't going out for a month. You want carry on with this Kel? I'll ban you for the rest of the year if you want."

"Fine, do what you bloody like, Dad. You and that witch of a mother just want to keep me miserable."

Martin inched ever closer to Kelly. She tasted the spittle from his mouth.

"What'd you call your mum? What'd you call her, you ungrateful slag?"

Kelly cowered under her father's wild eyes. She shivered when his hand withdrew and prepared herself for the unthinkable.

"Well, go on. What did you call her then?"

Tears bled into the mounts of mascara. Her father's strong hand held her captive.

"Martin, no."

A soft but firm hand took his right wrist and removed thoughts of corporal justice. Martin turned to find his wife easing him away from their errant daughter.

"Did you see that, Mum? Dad was going to hit me."

Stacey struck Kelly across her cheek. Shocked, she stumbled to the wall of the passage.

"And so he bloody well should. Look at you Kel, just bloody look at you."

Kelly's rebellious side surrendered to whimpered obedience. She eased her way to her bedroom in shock at the red mark on her face.

"First, no going out for a month. Second, no dressing up like a tart. Third, no fags. Fourth, no boozing. Fifth, no scummy mates. Sixth, no boys. Seventh, no music at all hours. Eighth, no telly in the bedroom. Ninth, you'll do what your mother tells you and tenth, you'll start to be a decent daughter again."

Her father's last commandment stabbed his daughter's heart. Martin always looked at her like she was number one. Now, the hag came between them and it hurt.

A pair of bewildered eyes glared back in disbelief.

"Dad, that's not fair. You can't do that, I'm fourteen for God's sake."

"I'll tell you what's not fair, you treating your mum and this place like trash. You have no idea just how hard she works to look after you and you repay her like this. Well, not any more, Madam."

Kelly smashed the door into its frame. Stacey restrained her husband from storming after her.

"Leave it, wait until morning. Let her realise what she's done."

He didn't speak. He exhaled hatred through his nose, and crashed into his chair.

"Martin, I just got one more thing to say to you though."

His wife took her place next to him on the settee.

"Thanks love. Thanks a million."

Their lips met. His rage subsided and thought hard about the taming of his wild daughter. He prayed his angel kept away from his own teenage path of self-destruction. He remembered the days of Joey and George. The road of nihilism always so alluring and rewarded him with gems of despair and heartache.

Chapter 21 Experimentation

"You sure you can come out, Kel? I thought your dad laid the law down."

The teenager snorted in indignation.

"As if. How's he going to stop me? Listen Trace, if you're having a party I want to be involved."

Tracey imagined a night without her wing lady. Kel brought animation, fun, vibrancy whilst Tracey brought organisation.

"That'd be great. Jase is going to be there as well."

"That's another reason I'm coming."

A fit of girlish giggling escaped the confines of the school corridor. An impatient teacher scowled his disapproval.

"Ladies, please try and maintain some form of control. This is supposed to be a place of learning, not a zoo."

The girls murmured their penitence and feigned innocence. Mr. Harris, unlocked the door and ushered his retinue inside.

"Who else is coming then, Trace?"

"Well, Amy, Kevin, Simon, Tiffany and Ian."

Kelly shrugged her shoulders in surprise.

"What did you want to bring Ian for? He's a tosser, Trace."

"He's Simon's best friend. If Simon don't come, then Tiffany won't either. You know what it's like."

"Well, you just make sure he doesn't bring a downer on it."

The two girls took their place at their desks and heeded the instruction to turn to page thirty-four and find the Yukon. Kelly's interest geography stopped at the end of the Old Kent Road.

"Don't worry. We'll get drunk and just have a good time. It's going to be a night we won't forget."

The teacher called out the names on the register. Kelly opened her exercise book and penned Friday:7:30 in the margin. She imagined her tongue in Jason's mouth and counted every second until the end of the day.

"Jase, all right lover?'

A boy with a head full of gel imbued spikes puckered at the sight of his girlfriend. A pair of slender arms took Kelly and their lips met.

"Hiya babes. How's my girl feeling today then?"

"Pissed off with the pair of half-wits I've got for parents. I'm going to cop it later, but I'm damned if I'm staying in watching my brother playing computer games and listening to my Mum going on and on. Besides, I want to be with you and have a bit of fun."

She quivered when his hand wandered near her posterior. His fingers tucked in just below the top of her dress.

"You two, time for plenty of that later. Mum and Dad haven't gone out yet."

The pair reddened in admonishment.

"Sorry Trace, but I've been looking forward to getting Jase to myself all week. It's all right for you, you ain't got Daddy Bear and Mummy Bear on your case."

"Fair enough, but they'll be gone soon. Go in the living room and watch the telly with Ian. He ain't so bad, you know."

"Yeah, right. Do I look like I work for care in the community or something?"

Jason grabbed a can of Stella whilst Kelly settled for carbonated vodka.

"Just humour me, will you? The others will be here soon enough."

Kelly followed her host and took residence on a lime velvet sofa. Ian offered a quiet hello.

"All right, mate." offered Jason. Kelly squirmed at her boyfriend's friendliness.

"Yeah, cheers, Jase. All right, Kel?"

"Suppose. What's on the box?"

"Something interesting about sharks. Well worth a watch actually."

Kelly glanced at her boyfriend. She hoped the others would arrive quick.

"Well, if you're into that sort of thing. Ain't there any music on anywhere? A bit boring just watching telly aint it?"

The boy curled his lip at Kelly's lack of interest.

"I suppose it is boring watching creatures getting ripped to shreds with blood gushing all over the screen. Course, if you think listening to some rabid chimp telling everyone to bust a move merits entertainment, then be my guest."

Kelly's stomach swelled in fury.

"Pardon me for fucking breathing. Listen mate, I haven't come here to watch the box all night, that's well sad."

"Kel, it's all right." said Jason.

"No, it bloody ain't." roared Kelly with her eyes blazing at her boyfriend's lack of backbone.

"Sorry, I didn't make myself clear, Kelly. I have brought, what you so happily call entertainment. Whilst the television is a decent medium to help whittle away the time, what I have in my bag will blow your minds, I assure you."

She ignored Ian's words. A stubby finger alighted on the off switch whilst her other hand hunted for a CD.

"Whatever, I'm sticking some tunes on."

Feral rave music soon burst from the speakers. Kelly struggled to hear the bass line. Once Tracey's parents departed things would liven up.

"Doesn't Tracey have anything a bit more captivating? "

Kelly ignored the cynic by the television. Her arms encircled Jason and she pulled him towards the centre of the room, determined to ignore the bugbear of the evening.

"You look bloody gorgeous, lover. Come here," teased Kelly.

Kelly kissed with all her vigour. She took delight with Ian's unease at their physical chemistry. Jason grabbed his girlfriend's buttocks. Teasing, before the grip became firmer, pulling her tight. She responded by reaching inside Jason's shirt, seeking out a stiffening nipple. A gentle tweak forced him to gasp.

"You two. can't you wait? Mum and Dad still ain't gone yet and if they came in here and caught you acting like that, I'd be right in the brown stuff."

The couple parted centimetre by centimetre and second by second. Tracey shook her head. Ian allowed himself an indulgent smirk.

"Sorry Trace, but the company in here ain't exactly the best, is it?"

"Couldn't agree with you more, Kelly, still, things will definitely get better later on, won't they Tracey?" retorted Ian.

Kelly took a note to hand Tracey a criteria for invitations in the future.

"Look, please try and get on you two. Ian's all right, really he is, he's just a bit different."

Tracey stood close to the anaemic wannabe vampire. Too close for Kelly's liking.

"Tell me you ain't, Trace."

"What? What you on about?"

Ian allowed the smirk on his face to grow ever wider.

"What, that me and Tracey are an item," beamed Ian in triumph.

Kelly's self-control failed and she lapsed into uncontrollable laughter, from sadness or hilarity, she could not be sure.

"What, boyfriend with him," she spat.

"Yeah, so what if I am?"

Tracey escaped when the doorbell sang. Jason squeezed his girlfriend's hand ever so soft.

"So how long has this been going on, then?"

Ian savoured every spiteful syllable. He stood equal in status to Kelly and Jason, a joke no more.

"I'd guess about three months now. And before you ask, yes, we have gone all the way. So many times now I've rather lost count."

Kelly struggled to digest his words. Her eyes betrayed the truth and bile contorted inside.

Tracey returned with Amy, Kevin, Tiffany and Simon.

"Hi, all right everyone," beamed an excitable Amy. Her boyfriend deferred to her superiority when she handed him her jacket.

"Good to see you Aims. Should be a scream tonight," said Kelly.

Ian reached besides his chair and took hold of a Tesco's bag.

"Sure will. It will be the biggest scream you lot have ever seen, won't it Simon?"

The small crowd followed Ian's gaze to Tiffany's boyfriend. Tiffany's concentration turned to a basilisk stare.

"What's he on about, Si?" enquired Jason.

Simon lapsed into silence. He waited for his friend of over five years to show the way.

"This of course," boasted Ian.

He teased the bag apart. In his hands lay a worn wooden case folded in two. He flicked the hinges and the letters of the alphabet ran around the board from A-Z. He picked up a small piece of arrowed plastic and lay it in the middle of the table.

"What the hell's that? Some sort of sprog's toy?"

Ian shot Tiffany a dark look.

"There really is no limit to some people's ignorance. Do any of you know what this is?"

Kelly knew. Her heart quailed in sudden dread.

"Put that bloody thing away. Bloody hell Trace, I want a night to remember, not that devil shit."

Tracey stared at the strange board, sharing Tiffany's ignorance.

"An Ouija board," offered Simon.

"Correct, with this thing we can talk to spirits can't we, Kelly?"

Ian enjoyed seeing his antagonist squirm.

"Tracey, don't fuck about with that crap. Let's just have some spliffs, booze and tunes yeah?"

Kelly's eyes narrowed in suspicion when Ian nodded.

"That's a damn good idea, Kelly. Let's get out of our minds first. If we make enough noise, we might just raise the dead."

A cheerful goodbye came from the passageway. Tracey's parents ready for their night out.

"See you later, Mum, Dad. Yeah, we'll be good," lied their daughter.

Loud drum and bass music swarmed inside the room at new intensity. Kelly seized a rolled piece of paper and enjoyed the cathartic effect of hemp. Her anxiety about the Ouija board faded. She melted in her boyfriend's arms, enjoying his amateurish groping skills. Several small empty bottles soon formed a ceremonial circle around Kelly and her friends. They indulged, fornicated and they worshipped the temple of hedonism.

Ian, did not. He sat with his girlfriend by his side, eyes fixed on Kelly's gradual decay into drunken oblivion. He glanced to his watch and found the hour of ten. Two hours his girlfriend's parents had been away. Two hours he had been forced to endure this display of decadent ennui. He stood, with no warning, walked to the speaker and switched off the stereo.

"What you doing?" said Jason.

Ian pointed to the Ouija board, sitting unmolested on a table. He took hold of the occult doorway, cleared a space in the middle of the floor and set it down. Ian ordered Tracey to dim the lights and place a candle in each corner of the room.

"Livening things up. Well, unless you're scared that is."

It was too easy to get people to follow his lead. Jason's bravado erupted.

"Scared of what? Some poxy letters? Sod off."

Ian pointed to a space by the Ouija board's right.

"Well, take your place then. The rest of you care to follow?"

Tracey sat at the head of the widening circle. Her friends followed, all sitting cross legged on the floor. One space remained.

"What's wrong, Kelly? You afraid?"

She sensed the dreaded power from the device. She swore the board quivered and shifted under her gaze. It almost looked alive.

"Look, I just ain't comfortable with that crap."

"She's terrified. What a pussy," gloated Ian.

Her friend's faces betrayed amusement. Fury rose, transformed to defiance.

"I'm not scared, I just don't see the point in fucking with that shit. We're here to party, for God's sake."

"Kelly is scared, Kelly is scared."

Ian's chorus inspired the others in the circle to join in with him. Even Jason joined in the taunting. Ian loved the control and her defiance conquered instinct. She took her place and took hold of Tiffany and Ian's hands. Latent energy flowed into her and she struggled to move.

"Well, then, let's see who's out there then, shall we?"

Ian pushed the planchette to the centre of the board.

"If there are any spirits out there, then please make your presence felt. We wish you no harm, merely respect. Please, if there is anyone is there, come forward."

At first, the board waited in insignificant stillness. Kelly, though, sensed an unwanted awakening within her. The same calling her father had, her grandmother shared, she did not belong.

She tried to stand. Her legs refused to obey. Ethereal chains held her and she looked on hopeless to the centre of the board. Iciness descended. Kelly struggled to breathe.

"My name is Ian. Please, we mean you total respect and honesty. If anyone is there, please let us know now."

A hoarse rasping alien groan breathed hard into Kelly's left ear. The presence exhaled onto her neck, freezing her throat.

A masculine energy encircled her. She writhed to her left, and in the darkness spotted a man of pensionable age coughing. He held a black cigarette in his right hand, laughing despite great pain. The others followed her gaze yet saw nothing. The wraith neared her neck, breathed out a rasping wheeze and his lips so close they could almost kiss her gentle windpipe.

"Who are you?" she asked.

The presence lurched towards the board. The planchette moved and wrote the letters, H, A, R, R, Y.

"Hello Harry. We're so pleased you came. If you don't mind, could you reveal your second name." ordered Ian.

The spirit stone did not stir. Ian, emboldened, asked a new question.

"Are you a friendly spirit?"

The planchette turned to the letters N and O.

Kelly tried to stand, the terror within threatened to take her last measure of composure.

"Do you mean us harm?"

The letters N and O came again. The group relaxed yet the planchette continued to move.

"No, not all of you. We want only one."

Kelly's shoulders crumpled under an unbearable weight. Her eyes stared harder at the Ouija board. She imagined it floated to the level of her eyes.

"You're not alone?"

The hoarse guttural reply needed no planchette. They all heard, "friends are with me."

"Who is with you then? Who do you want to hurt?"

The candles by their side experienced a rise in dark energy before dying out one by one.

A cup flew from the table and struck Kelly across the head. She fell, descended into a terrible gaol. Her face struck the Ouija board and she struggled to look up from within a dreadful gloom. She stood alone. A powerful grip dragged her to her feet.

She tried to close her eyes. The presence refused to allow her to comply. Her sight returned and in front of her stood Harry, laughing at the silly girl who dared to meddle.

He snapped her arms behind her back. Wraiths trapped her with black chains and her ankles were snared in similar fashion. Something beyond powerful hoisted her aloft. The creatures who so almost ensnared her father delighted in triumph.

She opened her mouth to scream yet no sound escaped. She sighed in defeat and the shadows took her down, ever down where hope never ventured to tread.

Chapter 22 Durance

Is this death? My friends, they seem so far away, so, so little and there's me going, going away into this place. What is this place? I'm confused as hell. That strange little hunchback man is looking at me well weird.

I'm almost starkers and the little perv is sticking his finger between a circle of his left index finger and thumb. Let him try and see what happens.

He tosses an ugly green jacket my way. I hate to think who had it last cause it reeks of lord knows what. I throw it on, at least I can hide my body.

I look around trying to make out this odd but familiar area. The hunchback points up; I make out a set of flats. It's where I live. I sprint as fast as my weak legs will go. Maybe Dad's in, maybe I'll stop being such an awful daughter to Mum. I'll make it up to her. At least Dad will sort out this fat creep who is following me with his dirty fag breath. I ain't ever ever seen anyone as ugly as him.

I get to the doors at the bottom and press my number waiting for Dad to pick up. Why doesn't he answer? Why ain't there anyone else around 'cause I never heard it as quiet as this? At last, static springs to the receiver.

"Dad, Dad it's me Kel. Let me in, will you?"

He doesn't answer. He must be well pissed at me. I can't blame him. He is going to go apeshit but I'm a girl of sixteen, not a ten-year old like he wants me to be. And like he was an angel at my age. I heard the stories about him failing at school, getting off his head on booze and shit. Well sod it, if he could do it, then I'm going to as well.

"Dad, let me in, I don't want to be out here in the cold."

"OK."

The voice sounds like Dad but something's not right. The hunchback doesn't follow me. I'm bloody relieved. He moves to the foyer doors though and breathes hard on them covering the glass with his phlegm, extending his tongue, licking it and his eyes glaze over. I'm up the stairs, not bothering with the lift cause everyone knows it don't work.

I run up to the sixth floor. It doesn't take long and my door lies open. I'm going to get it big time but at least I'll be back home. Yeah, I'll be different now, I'll start acting better instead of being a horrible slag.

It's so dark. I wonder if the leccy has gone again. There's always something going wrong in these poxy flats. I barge in, and I can see three distant shapes. Mum, Dad and my little brother.

"Sorry I'm late, Dad. I didn't think I'd be out so long. I know you're annoyed with me but I won't do it again, I promise."

His shape stumbles towards me. Something really isn't right.

"I know you won't, pretty. You won't be going anywhere."

That's not my Dad. Oh God, what is going on? I'm running to the door, but it's sealed. My frantic hands scrabble about and latch onto where the handle should be. Nothing. Just a slab of cold wood, sealing me in.

"Let me out. Let me out."

I'm screaming loud as I can. No-one's listening. I feel his hot breath on my neck. I turn, eager to push this stranger away but he catches my arm, pushes me towards the living room.

"You just came in here by your own choice. Why would we want to let you out? We've got to keep a close eye on you, ain't we, Kelly Lowe?"

His voice dreadful, like he's gobbling a dozen marbles in a jar covered in treacle. His tongue flaps back and forth on the top of his mouth. His giggling family don't say a word. The little sprog shuffles over to the corner, hits a switch on the box and a purplish smoke lights up the room, only a bit though. Enough for me to see these stunted arseholes who keep me prisoner.

Shadowfruit

What a bunch of pricks.

The first, who I thought was my Dad, must be about five foot eight. He's big like Dad, but not from muscle. Hasn't shaved for days. His hair running away from his forehead and eyebrows are bushy tufts of mouldy hair. The eyes hold a couple of piggy white spots and it's too dark to tell what colour they are. I bet they're black. He's wearing a t-shirt and on it is written 'scum.' My stomach churns. His belly flops over the top of a pair of stripy moth eaten boxer shorts. He's wearing a pair of holey socks and a pair of sandals showing a pair of feet ridden with gout. And I thought the hunchback was ugly.

I release the contents of my stomach, covering the floor with a sorry green puke.

"Well, waste not want not, son."

The one I thought was my brother is on his knees. No he can't, stop it, he frigging is. The little bastard laps up my innards like a dog eating Winalot. His tongue, black from bile soaks up my dreadful treasure. He offers me a toothy grin, well it would be if he had teeth, and points to his mum.

Mum. Oh hell, this woman hates me. I sense it, her eyes wild, her face contorted. She grabs my hair with no warning and twists my neck down.

"Thought you'd stay out all night, did you? Thought you'd let your mates have their way with you? Thought you'd get off your face on lord knows what. Mummy knows, you know. I know everything about you, slut."

"Let me go. You're not my Mum."

She leathers me across my cheek with her palm. My lips bleed, she forces me to stand.

"Ungrateful slag, not your mum? I'll show you, I'll bloody show you."

She rips off my jacket, exposing me. The two males laugh and point but she isn't interested in molesting me. She sits her strong body on a sofa and holds me captive across her knee.

"You need discipline and you need it now. Ain't your mum, how dare you."

I scream when her hand thumps tender flesh. The bitch scratches, raking up blood, knowing it'll hurt.

"Hit her good, Mummy. Make her bleed, make her sing."

"Yeah go on Lacey, punish her."

The son and husband get real close. Her hand falls on me again and again. My backside is on fire, my blood spills onto her hands. It goes on forever. I'm in so much agony and I don't know where I am. She stops, offers her fingers to her husband who licks my blood. These sadistic vampires, sit me up, stick me in the middle of their sofa whilst they sit beside me and start stroking me like I'm a cat they've caught. Surrogate dad on my left, Lacey on my right and sprog on Lacey's lap.

"Oh Mum, that was beautiful. Why'd you stop though? I wanted her skin ripped off, you know I love a good skinning."

She pats the boy on the head with her strange love.

"Orders from the boss, darling. Wants us to look after her. Oh look, our favourite programme is on."

An image starts takes form on the phosphorous box and a familiar unwanted face smiles at me. It's dreadful to see him in his best clobber, this creep who came and took me over.

"It's Harry Hunchback, Ma. Wonder if we'll make it on the box. It'd be fucking ace."

"Oi, watch your language pup."

The smiler leers at us from the back of the screen.

"Welcome one and all to News Den. And what a fantastic day we've had. Our takings have risen to a special high after one of our agents, well, actually it was me, went and caught a newbie and what a hottie she is."

The image of the Hunchback falls away. A covert camera narrows in on me, it isn't over here though- it's back at the other place with me joining hands at the table, only the camera isn't taking the picture from where I am, it's following me from over where I am now. God, it's confusing.

"This is it everyone, this is where I get called to the party. Have you ever seen such a bunch of complete tossers in charge of a Ouija board? Mate, it's easier than taking a rusk of a baby. Hold on, watch this part, this is where I go in and shake them up."

He steps through the veil we opened. He strides up to my side before he fiddles with that planchette telling us he means us harm.

"Oh boy, you can smell their fear, can't you and look at my target. Kelly Lowe is her name and thanks to me I've got her all secure with her new family."

"Hey Mum, Dad, that's us."

My kidnappers' photos rush on screen. I shrivel when I see the terrible images of a right rotten family. It's so bad I almost wish I was back with Harry Hunchback. My adopted mum scares me the most though. Hard faced, unsmiling and a scar across her left cheek is the snapshot she offers.

"Yes people, it's our good friends the Coes. What a fine down-standing lot they are. I've got to tell you, young Kelly couldn't have found a more uncaring bunch of bastards if she tried."

The camera pans out with the Hunchback tangling his hands in my hair, dragging me across the fold of the physical plane into this hellish place. I see myself half naked, running away with Harry right behind me, smacking my arse, guffawing, pointing and urging me to this set of flats.

"Oh these silly children who think they know it all, eh citizens? Running off at the mouth at how hard they are, how nasty they can be, blah, blah, bluddery blah. Pah! Well young Kelly Lowe, I mean Coe, you've come to the right place. The only way out of here you hard-nosed lily white baby, is for Daddy to come and take your place."

A picture of my dad by my bedside in hospital flashes on the screen. There's a right bunch of evil sods just out of his eye line, pointing at him, drawing their fingers across dark throats with yellow and red eyes blazing.

"Soon he'll try and come for Daddy's little girl and there'll be no Nanny Nan to help him this time. He's going to come alone and we're going to have him. Oh yeah, he'll be right at home with his daughter round the Coes, don't you think?"

Shut up I scream. Screw my surrogate family, I want my dad, I want him now.

"Shut your cakehole. It's time for your bed."

Mama Coe's right hand smacks my cheek. I lose balance, my bastard little brother tripped me and he's tickling my soles and toes. The father's there too, grabbing my arms and together they hoist my body aloft.

"Time to treat this dog like she deserves."

Lacey yanks something out from behind the settee. No way are they putting me in there. I scream and shout, kicking and take comfort when the ball of my foot kicks my wraith brother under the chin. Dad Coe is losing his grip. I bring my leg up and stamp hard down on his shin. She hits me again. No mucking around this time. My rage nothing compared to her strength and with no effort, she hurls my tiny body over her shoulder.

"Open the door and get this vixen all snug for the night."

A portal of wire is pulled back. There's no way I'll fit in there. A heavy set of palms say otherwise. Her fingers grip my shoulders, nip at my ribs and prod me down below. She forces me inside bit by bit with Dad and little Coe laughing at my puny struggles. My body can't breathe. The cow holds my ankles and pushes down with all her weight. My feet bend behind my knees and the door shuts with my soles on fire.

God it hurts. Unbreakable chicken wire nibbles at my every pore. Lacey grabs a wooden handle atop of my new home and hoists me onto the table.

"There you go, just like a good little poodle now, ain't she?"

Little brother prods me through the gaps in the wire of my metal kennel.

"Her skin's all soft, ain't it Mum? How comes that?"

Twisted Dad yanks at one of my toes through the wires.

"Well son, she thinks she's still got hope. It won't last. Soon her body will be blackened and cracked like the rest of us and she won't be so high faluting then, will she?"

"Let me out, you bunch of pricks. What kind of sad bastards are you?"

Lacey storms to the head of the cage, jabbing her finger towards my eyes.

"Oi young lady, best you start obeying some ground rules around here. First, if there's any profaning round here it'll come from me, not the likes of a stuck up slag like you. Second, when you're in the cage you will shut up. Third, you don't get out of there until we think you start showing us a bit more respect, especially seeing as we hold the cards now. Are you getting the picture, dearie?"

"Fuck off."

I'm going to suffer for that. So be it, the day they break my defiance is the day I know it's no longer worth sticking around. Let her do her worst.

She doesn't disappoint.

I expect her to start pinching and nipping at me again. I see her instead grab the hoover and picks up some sort of wiry thing.

"Kids, always have to learn the hard way, don't they love?"

Her husband's solemn head nods.

"You better let me out of here. I swear I'll beat the crap out of all of you."

My body is engulfed by a blue fire. Every part of me twitches in blinding captivity. I scream, again, again and again and again. All the while Lacey Coe giggles before inserting her choice of amusement. It gets me everywhere. Toes, calves, soles of me feet, thighs, face and everywhere. All the while she carries on electrocuting me.

"Bet you're feeling plenty energetic now, ain't you? Fancy screaming a bit more?"

This time she goes for it. I want to scream stop, yet the words don't come. All I do is release the air in my lungs in a shriek. A flash. Must be the electricity. No. There it is again. Is it lightning?

"That's it, I'll take another picture of her. Look at her getting all sweaty. Go on Mama, hit her again."

The agony returns. My eyes weigh heavy and my heart is ready to burst. Can you die in hell?

"That's a good one for the family album son. She's even more fun than the last one we had in here. God what was her name again, Lace?"

"Damned if I know and as if I care. We got a new pet, all courtesy of Harry Hunchback. He's a top presenter, ain't he?"

"Very nice of you to say so, Lacey. Oh, I see you've got our new recruit all nice and snug. Hope you're not treating her well."

They've let him in. That bastard who caught me. Harry bloody Hunchback, curse his slug of a heart.

"Ooh, look at her, all that old fight has gone right out of her, Lace. You've done a damn good job already."

His finger jabs me through the holes, in the cage, exploring and probing. I scream, I want to wake up, this isn't funny anymore.

"Ah, doesn't she sing so well? Listen dear Coe family, I'm going to take your little pet on a journey. The Guvnor wants to give her the once over, you know, see if she really is cut from the same cloth as her dad."

Shadowfruit

My new prison rises. There must be a handle on top of this human cage. I piss myself. The trickle runs down my leg and dribbles onto the floor below where twisted brother runs and he licks his lips.

Harry ruffles the boy's hair and prods me again, urging me to empty my bladder some more. I'm not sure what is in me, I mean if I'm in some weird plane or whatever you want to call it. How can I be hungry? How can I be thirsty?

His fingers squeeze me and he purrs in delight.

"Good girl, good girl. Nice to see you're settling in Kelly."

I'd puke again if I could. My throat is too raw from the release of atrabilious gunk from earlier. My surrogate mum opens the door and foul air mixes with the corrupt atmosphere in here. I glimpse a corpulent foot from my step father and his hand stroking himself on the thigh.

"Bring her back real soon, Harry. You know she's family now."

He says goodbye. I bounce to and fro in my cage, his fast pace making me wince in pain from the chicken wire. Several forms scuttle away when Harry comes near. They peer at me from behind yellow stained pillars. Some point and laugh, others lick their lips while most look down desperate to avoid the attentions of the devil who holds me. They need not worry tonight, or is it today? No, his attention is fixated upon one object tonight, little old me.

"Right, let's get the old jalopy fired up and see what the big man's got to say. I reckon he's going to be quite taken by you."

A door to some kind of four by four lurches open and he stuffs me end up on the back seat. I find myself almost standing. He prods me a couple more times.

"Hmm, nice, fresh and juicy. Just the way the boss likes 'em. Shame your innocence has gone, but still, you're more than acceptable."

He creeps into the driver's seat. There's some moody tunes from the sixties being piped out of his radio and I have a sensation of floating. I twist my head and peer out of the windscreen and see no road before us. Ahead of us lay clouds, the moon and darkness.

"What, you think we drive on the roads here? Silly. No road goes to where I'm taking you gorgeous, we've got to fly up there."

I'm expecting a journey of hours but my eyes refuse to close. My mind wanders in the solace of memory yet my concentration is interrupted when the car crunches to a halt.

"We're here. Not far to his quarters, not long before he gives you the once over."

I want to get out. All I can muster is a little pitter patter on the cage, amusing the hunchback to pitiful huffs of mirth.

A purplish haze envelops us. I'm looking down to an unwashed chequerboard floor. We wander until we come to a black, gold and red metal door.

"Come in, Harry," roars a voice, not unlike a teacher I've heard.

I rise and my cage nestles on something. For goodness sake, it's a pedestal. My prison is turned and a new set of eyes examine me. I don't want to look even when he says I ought to be released from the cage. A metal flap opens and the hunchback grabs my ankle. He yanks my leg, stuffing me into the light. A soothing voice tells Harry to stop and a gentle yet powerful hand touches the base of my chin and tilts my head up.

I look deep into the eyes of pure evil.

Chapter 23 Helpless

He stumbled into a realm of confusion, disbelief and panic. She'd been a pain but her grades were improving, her application for college successful and she liked a good time. Stacey complained, yet his daughter contained that persistent Lowe defiant streak and his love for her beat ever strong.

He bulldozed into a ward full of drips, nurses and stressed doctors.

"Kelly, what's happened to you darling?"

He sat by his daughter's side. He grabbed her hand to force his warmth into her own.

"I'm sorry, are you related to this young lady?"

A fervent nod followed.

"I'm her father. What's happened?"

A white coated guardian eased Martin away from his daughter.

"If you come with me I'll explain. My name is Dr. Pastor, and you are?"

"Martin Lowe."

"Martin, please, follow me."

A sterile white door opened into a small office. The doctor instructed his guest to take a chair next to a desk buried in folders and notes.

"Is she going to be all right?"

Dr. Pastor sat opposite and sighed.

"I'm afraid at this time we don't know. We're running tests but your daughter is in a state of unconsciousness."

"But how? What the fuck happened? Sorry Doc."

Dr. Pastor brokered no offence. He'd heard far worse in Lewisham hospital.

"Well, unfortunately the details are more than vague. A young couple told us they were having a party and she collapsed."

Martin's eyes swelled in white fury.

"She didn't just collapse. The idiots probably stuck her full with happy pills. Where are they? I'll find out."

Martin's hands transformed into hammers of destruction primed for action

"They're with the police who are taking statements. Look, I'll level with you Martin, you need to focus on your daughter. Let the authorities do their job."

Martin slumped in his chair.

"So if it's drugs you can sort her out then?"

The doctor shook his head.

"We don't know. Yet something about this tells me this isn't about drugs. Her body functions are fine, it's just that she has fallen into a comatose state."

"Coma?"

"I'm afraid so. Comas are somewhat of an enigma, Martin. Sometimes the patient recovers in a few hours, days or weeks. Unfortunately, it isn't always the case."

"You mean she might not wake up again?"

A reluctant nod followed.

"It is a possibility, but we'll do all we can to bring your daughter back. In the meantime, you can help as well, you and all your family."

Martin supped on tea to soothe his harsh voice.

"How? Anything, I can do and it's done."

"Talk to her, hold her hands, tell her stories, Martin. You'll be amazed what an affect it can have on the patient."

"Course, course. Cheers Doctor, I'll do that. Can I start now?"

Dr. Pastor rested his hand on Martin's shoulder for the merest of moments.

"We'll tell you when you can. Let us carry out our tests and as soon as we're done, you can be with her. For now, I'll ask you to go to the reception desk."

Martin pleaded to stay. The doctor held sway though. He trudged back defeated and heartbroken along a disinfected hallway. A pleasant nurse little older than his daughter met him.

"Is there anything I can get you, Mr. Lowe?"

He brushed away sweat from his brow. He checked his watch for some absurd reason and walked to and fro in a state of total impotence.

"Mr. Lowe, another cup of tea? Something to eat maybe?"

Martin's attention turned to a small piece of plastic.

"Oh for fuck's sake."

The nurse flinched at his outburst.

"Sorry?"

"No, I'm sorry love. Look, can I borrow your phone?"

Martin's fingers gripped the handle before she responded.

"Sure, press nine for an outside line."

He beat a tune on the digital keypad.

"Hello?"

"Babe, it's me. Has anyone told you about, Kelly?"

"No. Mart, what you on about?"

"No-one told you, they didn't call you?"

"Martin, you're worrying me now. What's happened? Where's our Kel? She's all right, ain't she?"

"No babe, she's not."

His voice disintegrated struggling to find a thread of coherence.

"Babe, what's happened? Tell me!"

The nurse offered her hand. Martin gave her the receiver and collapsed onto a chair in total misery.

"Hello, Mrs. Lowe, it's Lewisham Hospital here. Yes, your husband was talking to you. Unfortunately, your daughter is with us. Yes, of course you can come down. We'll tell you more details when you arrive. She was involved in an incident. My name is Nurse Gibson."

The nurse looked to Martin who reclaimed the phone.

"Why the bloody hell didn't you tell me she was in hospital? What's going on?"

"Sorry babe, just get down here love and tell my Mum. I need you, Kelly needs you."

His voice cracked again.

"I'll be as quick as I can."

The phone died. Martin, sat back and cried.

Fifteen minutes passed to twenty. His daughter still kept away from him and the helplessness inside grew in impatience. Nurse Gibson offered him the perpetual solace of the gift of pity.

"Mart, what's happened to our baby?"

The frustration of the last couple of years with her daughter vanished when she saw his tear-stained face.

"She's in a coma babe. I'm not sure what happened but the Docs are running tests. Might be drugs, booze, anything."

Stacey shook her head, disbelief etched onto her face.

"But I told her not to go out. I should never have left her alone, should have been there."

Her body bobbed on Martin's chest.

"Don't be silly babe. She would have got out sooner or later, we both know that. I just want to get my hands on the little bastards who were with her."

"Who was with her? Where did she go then? What's she gotten into, for God's sake?"

Her husband shrugged.

"The police are finding out. I don't know what's going on except our daughter is in a really bad way."

Stacey's vision brightened at the sight of a doctor heading towards them.

"Mrs. Lowe?"

She nodded.

"I'm not sure if your husband has told you but I am treating your daughter."

"Is she going to be all right?" her parents said in unison.

"Well, the good news is that she is stable. Her heart beat is regular and all other vital signs are normal."

Martin seized the glimmer of hope.

"Is she is going to wake up then? When, how long?"

The Doctor ran his palm through his balding head.

"That brings us to our current problem, I'm afraid. She should be in a perfect situation to regain her consciousness, yet remains in a comatose state."

"So you don't know then? What about drugs? Are there any in her system? Maybe when they're gone she'll come round."

"There were minute traces of marijuana and alcohol in Kelly's bloodstream Mr. Lowe, but nothing that should cause this."

Stacey's hand grabbed her husband's fingers.

"So what happens now? You just going to sit and watch?" barked an exasperated Stacey.

"Observation is certainly a tool we will use. However, if there is no physical reason for her to remain in a coma it makes me think of another area to explore, meaning her mental state."

Martin's rage simmered to dangerous levels.

"You saying our daughter's a nutjob?"

Stacey's easer her hand onto Martin's shoulder

"It's all right babe, they're trying their best."

"We are not making any conclusions at this time Mr. Lowe, merely looking at all possible reasons for her current situation. What concerns me is she may have been exposed to some kind of trauma which caused this current condition."

"Trauma? What trauma? She only had a bit of booze and puff."

"We can't say at this time Mr. Lowe. It just looks to me as though Kelly may have lapsed into a coma to escape something. At this early stage it is all conjecture, of course."

Martin's darkest imagination conjured insidious thoughts of depravity.

"If anyone's laid a finger on her, I'll rip their heart out. What are the Old Bill doing about it, sitting on their arses?"

The doctor shrugged.

"I'm afraid I can't speak for the police, Martin. However, if you wish, you can go through to see your daughter again. Remember, talk to her, tell stories, tell jokes, anything you think might help."

Kelly's parents weren't listening. They sprinted down the corridor, into the ward where their daughter lay.

"Kelly, darling it's me, Dad. Where are you? Come back from wherever you've gone."

Martin grabbed her left hand, Stacey her right.

"Kel, forget about all that stuff we said the other day. We'll get it sorted out, I promise. Come on, come back here."

Stacey's cheeks were awash with unchained tears at the sight of her daughter sleeping like a lost Rapunzel.

Martin kissed his daughter's fingers, continued to talk, his wife joining in to bring their child back from oblivion.

"Mr and Mrs Lowe?"

Martin looked up to the alien female voice. A figure in black awaited.

"I'm W.P.C Samuels. Could you come with me, there's a few things we need to discuss."

Martin left his daughter with great reluctance. He thundered after the policewoman and prayed she'd have answers.

The doctor offered the constable the use of his office. She sat and invited Martin and Stacey to follow suit.

"Do you have any idea why your daughter was out this evening, Mr. Lowe?"

"She was grounded, Officer. We told her not to go anywhere. Do you know what's going on, or what?"

Joanne Samuels raised her hands in placation.

"Forgive me Mr. Lowe, Mrs. Lowe, but we're just trying to get all the facts. We think we do have some idea as to what happened but anything you can tell us could help the investigation considerably."

Stacey found her voice, conquering her emotions.

"Look, I know you've a job to do and that but could you just tell us what you know. Last time I saw her, she was pissed off and watching the box. And now she's in there like that."

Stacey swayed on her seat, her husband threw his arms around her.

"Well, I'm afraid the details are a bit vague but it seems your daughter went to a party along with several of her friends. I understand it was Tracey who arranged this."

"Just wait when I get hold of the scuzzy little mare," growled Stacey.

"You let us worry about her, Mrs. Lowe. Anyway, as I was saying, your daughter had a few drinks, some marijuana and lots of loud music. It was your standard teenager bit of fun except for one thing we didn't expect."

"What?" implored Martin.

"An Ouija board. It seems they were holding a seance and it was at around this time when Kelly became unconscious."

Martin reeled at the word Ouija board as though shot by psychic bullets. He knew what lurked in the dark corners of the unseen world. He knew the machines would be useless. His blackest depths of imagination conjured a new figure. A familiar shadow laughed and it possessed his daughter, utterly, completely. He knew the beast wanted him.

He bit his lip. All the years of fleeing from his cursed gift came to this point and he visualised a path of total darkness into the heart of their realm, twisted, dark, cruel and there he'd find him and his sadistic allies.

"I'll see you soon Kelly, I promise. See you soon." He kissed her brow and held her hand tighter than ever before.

Chapter 24 Can Somebody Help?

Martin's skin shivered in slithers of cold energy. He hadn't dabbled for so long. He wondered how much things had changed since he last danced in the veil. He remembered the panic when he lost touch with reality and almost drowned in that terrible place. He remembered those phantom ziggurats of dire emotion. Martin sat in front of a mirror and remembered his dead grandmother.

Total silence consumed the lounge. He stared unseeing into the silver window. In his mind he called out.

"Nan, are you there? Nan, can you help me?"

Did the mirror ripple? He wasn't sure. A dark scent of decay arose around him. Martin ignored the reek. He continued to stare, continued to call out. The room darkened and the sound of squalid whispers grew from within.

"Nan, I need you. My daughter needs you, can you please help?"

The mirror buckled, warped in on itself and a parody of Martin stared back. The creature's eyes blazed red, then yellow.

It stared back from a mirrored room of its own. Instead of a television stood an oven, inside it something furry squealed for release. His apparition roared in unheard laughter, turned a knob and ignited his dinner. The beast trailed old spittle down its chin, salivating at the feast to come. Martin snapped his attention to the unfortunate creature inside. He thought it to be a cat from the sound it made, but no. It was humanoid, red, not furry but hairy. The denizen beat upon white hot bars with no hint of release. Flesh seared, fat boiled and liquids dried.

Martin's twin turned up the heat and Martin sensed the fiend's mind. Better to be well done than half alive. His double shuffled over to the stove, seized an ankle and threw the meat onto a dining table. He severed the leg with one blow from a cleaver and to Martin's immense disgust raised it to the mouth of its vanquisher.

Flesh and sinew left bone devoured. The cleaver fell again in the awful spectacle of carving and eating. Bit by bit the carcass disappeared until the head remained.

The fiend scooped out blackened brain with a wooden spoon, feasted on old memories, salivated on incinerated nerves and gorged on dismembered neural pathways.

Martin fought hard to tear himself from the darkness. He prayed his daughter might come forward and he'd let her know Daddy was coming.

The creature cast aside the rest of its repast, reading Martin's thoughts. It called out, yet the whole scene remained in silence. A shuffling harridan appeared next to her corrupt husband and laid a greasy palm on his shoulder. The pair exchanged surreptitious words and a red glint formed in her black eyes. She pointed. Martin followed her lead, towards the corner. A cage awaited where an eager boy inserted a wooden stick.

Martin thoughts jived into all thoughts of dire consequence. The parents brought the cage nearer. The boy prodded something white. The wood pierced a female trammelled in a hutch of razor wire.

Her young blood ran through the gaps. The boy lapped up her essence. Martin's warped wife pointed to the head of the cage. A terrified face in sufferance started when the glint of metal illuminated her darkness. She fidgeted in the ridiculous tight space, a slave to the torment of the family who took joy in her brutalisation. Martin held back his tears no more.

"I'm coming for you, Kel. They can't keep you there. They can't stop me."

She did not hear. Kelly froze when her step-mother reached into the opening and seized her adopted daughter by the jaw. Her mouth jarred open and her mother filled it with insidious gruel. His twisted double pointed to her stomach, then to the oven. Stuff her, roast her and eat her.

Martin begged the creatures to stop. They paid no heed, continued to pour meat into her gullet. He cried out for his Grandmother again, praying she would come.

"No chance. She's gone to that world of light. She can't help your little slut now, no-one can." The cold voice poisoned his hopes. No-one stood next to him, yet he knew the veracity of the statement.

"Let her go, you bastards. Why don't you come and fight me?"

They paid him no heed. They continued to torment his daughter, eager to inflame his hysteria. He stared no more. Why did they take his daughter? She was nothing to them.

He confronted the cur of denial. She was everything to them. She made the perfect bait to call him to their world again.

He looked back to the mirror. The looking glass revealed his gaunt face. He needed help and threw himself into his chair.

The South London Press fell off the arm, opening itself to the middle pages. Martin, picked the paper up and his gaze fell to a small advert. His fingers glowed when his eyes alighted on the words medium, reach your loved ones and help those find the light. His eyes lingered on the corniest name he had ever seen for a psychic; a name he would dismiss but not today. His mind told him this woman might help.

The last month of Kelly's interminable sleep was the longest of times. He punched in the numbers and waited. A gentle Nigerian voice answered and he caught his breath.

"Hello."

"Hello, is that Mary Celestial?"

"What is it, child? Do you need my help?"

"I've lost my daughter."

"Has she passed over or still in the physical?"

"Neither, she's in limbo."

There was a pause. He wondered if this a bad mistake, his hand wavered near the end call button.

"Kelly is in trouble, of that there is no doubt. The worst kind, but you already know this."

His breath caught in his throat. His mind throbbed at Mary's impossible words.

"Those that have her mean to hurt her really bad. They are soul thieves of the worst kind and their master is the lord of all darkness. You know this, for you've been there before."

"How? Have you been following me?"

"How can I follow a man who rang me out of nowhere? We need to talk."

His nose discerned a sudden burst of the scent of mangoes and violets. The aroma dispelled the terrible stench, invigorated his spirit and donated the gift of hope.

"It sounds a good idea. Mind you, how much do you charge? I'm not made of money."

A hearty laugh filtered back through his earpiece.

"Nor am I. Don't you worry about money. I never charge up front and ask a fee. I leave that up to you if you're satisfied with my work."

"Sounds too good to be true."

"That's my terms. Take it or leave it. I swear to you, you only pay what you think my work is worth."

Martin pondered. He needed help wherever it came, even from the likes of Mary Celestial. He gave no hint of his daughter's peril and she came straight to the point, perhaps she might have some suggestions.

"Well, you did seem to know about Kelly. All right, I'll meet you."

The receiver warmed in his hand. He dismissed the sensation, sure it was coincidence.

"I hope I can help you. Tell me your name."

"I thought you was a clairvoyant, medium or whatever you call yourself."

The laughter returned, her good nature chilling the doom around him.

"You can call me what you like. I can make contact with your daughter because she straddles two plains. But you here on the ground, I can't read you except I think you had the gift once. In fact, you still do."

Martin stared at the phone. Every word she spoke confirmed her authenticity.

"Yeah. When I was young, I turned away from that nonsense."

Mary's voice darkened, the light mien of her voice faded to fearful solemnity.

"You know it's not nonsense. Listen well. You need to open up again, because you have to face them."

He shrank at the thought of seeing the shadows face to face. "It's OK to be scared. A man would be mad not to be, but you're not alone. There is help out there if you know where to look. There are those wonderful being smore than capable of sending them shadows into the darkest corners. Your grandmother knew that."

Martin's brow furrowed in astonishment.

"How did you know about her?"

"I can see the other side. It's my gift. Now when are you going to come and visit me?"

"I don't know. The sooner the better, I guess."

He heard a sudden burst of pages turning.

"Well, I could fit you in tomorrow. Is one o'clock convenient?"

"I think so, yeah of course it is."

"Good, I look forward to seeing you."

"Thank you."

The laughter returned, brightening the mood once again.

"I didn't know you were a clairvoyant as well."

Martin started at the receiver in confusion.

"Sorry? What'd you mean?"

"Two things, my address and maybe you could tell me who you are?"

Martin shrugged with embarrassed laughter.

"How silly of me. My name's Martin Lowe."

"Thanks Martin, my address is Thirty-Nine Clapton House. It's not far from the school, do you know it?"

"I think so, although haven't been down that way for ages."

"Oh and one other thing.'

"What?"

The radiance in Mary's voice burned louder than ever.

"Don't allow yourself to get down or upset. That sound of laughter you just gave me is a weapon to make those beasts run for their sorry lives. Remember that, remember the goodness in you and believe."

Martin struggled to remember the last time he had the strength to succumb to happiness.

"What about my Grandmother? You said she knew how to help, can't we ask her?"

"Not any more, Martin. You know full well she walked through the light."

He closed his eyes remembering how lost he felt in their realm. She had come for him then. How on Earth was he supposed to battle them now?

"Martin, she might not be able to help you but I can. Others can and we will do all we are able to ask for their help."

"I suppose so."

"There's no suppose about it. Now take my advice and have a good meal, a nice sleep and dream of the power of light. Don't let those clouds take hold."

Martin sensed a warm aura cosset his shoulders. He found solace and strength from the smell of the sea breeze along with the scent of geraniums and lavender.

"I'll do my best. And Miss Celestial?"

"Call me, Mary. Between you and me, Celestial isn't really my second name you know."

Laugher escaped between them again.

"Thanks for everything. I mean it."

"Thank me when we've got Kelly back, Martin. Now, you rest up and get ready for tomorrow."

Chapter 25 Dark Journey

He lost count of the years since he last travelled to this lost world. His awareness tumbled forward with each slow step to an old haunt.

To anyone else, Thirty-Nine Clapton House looked unremarkable. Green doors long in need of paint teemed in ubiquitous geometry across the estate. Mary Celestial's entrance adopted the same sombre appeal, yet Martin discerned incredible radiance flowing to the sky, warming the receptive side of him, eager to help.

He brushed past several youths on the stairs, eyeing him up, daring him to speak. The ascent continued and the reek of urine, spilt beer and vomit filled the atmosphere with their redolent bouquet of nausea. He recalled previous donations of his own returning to him with a touch of guilt

He reached the third floor, peered to his left. A huddle of small children swarmed outside his destination. The boys and girls stopped playing, stood as one and stared. A boy, hair almost shaved puffed out cheeks and chest, defiant and strong despite his nine years.

Martin cowered. The boy possessed something formidable within him and he baulked at approaching his domain. Martin shielded his abdomen as if to ward off an attack, instead, the shirtless child inserted his tiny right hand into Martin's sweaty palm.

"Are you Martin Lowe?"

The adult nodded, uneasy of the ring of children around him.

"Well you must come in. My Mum, I mean, Mary Celestial is waiting for you."

The barricade of young bodies parted. Martin followed his guide inside, past a staircase, above which a young baby screamed for attention.

"Hush up, Joseph. You just have to wait a bit. Mum's busy, so just hush up."

The baby paid no heed. The boy clicked his teeth before leading Martin on.

"All that boy does is moan. I never went on like that."

The boy pushed open a cream door missing its skirting. A strong voice chastised the boy at once.

"You are damn right, Patrick. You were never like that; you were far worse. Now you go and take this to your brother and make sure he eats it all."

"You mean drink."

Patrick took possession of a bottle of white and also a swift rap across the skull.

"Ow."

"Don't you try and be smart with your mum."

The boy's bravado dissipated with the smack. He sped past Martin with tears welling up and scampered to his little brother.

"Please come in Martin, and I'm sorry my boy was so cheeky. These little ones, they have no respect."

Martin observed his benefactor and guide, for some reason he expected her to be largesse and draped in flowing robes. Instead, a woman, sleek, elegant and dressed in a long purple dress took his hand. Her skin perfect black, her touch light, warm, wise and inquisitive. He turned his face towards hers and eyes of teak radiance stared straight into him.

"My, my, Martin, it's not often I see someone as bright as you."

He looked to the floor in embarrassment.

"You don't get many white people visit you then?"

She laughed. Her giggle infectious, soothing yet powerful.

"Don't be silly. Of course I do. No, I'm talking about what's in you. I've never seen such a light since way back home. Now I see why they covet you so much, they want you for their own."

The sudden malice in her voice unsettled Martin.

"Forgive me, I should watch my words, even if they be true. Come, sit down and let me get you a drink. We have a lot of talking to do."

She ushered him to a sofa. She cast aside a green throw. He deposited his frame and fidgeted whilst an errant spring did its utmost to dislodge him.

"Do you want a cup of tea or coffee, Martin? Maybe something stronger, although perhaps that should wait till later. Much later actually. Just stick to tea or coffee for now."

"Cup of tea please, Miss Celestial."

"Oh please, just Mary. Let's leave the Celestial nonsense to those who need convincing. I know you don't. I know you can see, see more than you can ever believe."

Martin wrinkled his nose.

"I'm just a bloke who drives a van, Mary. Just a bloke who is a crap father."

"Not at all," chimed a voice from the kitchen. "You just give your girl a bit too much freedom, that's all. Dad's do it all the time, but then, most dads don't have the Abiku to worry about."

"Who?"

"They are the ones that have your daughter and invited by him. They're dark twisted demons attracted to the light and dark. Light so they can corrupt it and feed on it. The dark, they pray on to make them stronger. Those in endless night become their slaves, their pleasure and give them their life."

"Kelly, oh God, no, is that was she is now? Is she their dark pet," cried Martin.

I'll not lie to you. That's exactly where she is. She's at the edge of death. And be of no doubt, if she dies in their grip, your daughter will be theirs. It is a hard fight and the odds are against us and what we can do is limited."

Martin rose from his chair.

"Where do you think you're going?"

"You said we can't do a thing about it. So why the fuck am I here?"

Martin paused by the door with rage and hope battling inside his own shattered thoughts.

"Now you listen, Mister. Don't you ever raise your voice or use bad words in my house again. Don't you understand anything yet?" Her voice powerful, commanding and without question. His stomach swam with nausea and tears flowed.

"I'm sorry, I didn't mean to swear at you but you said it's hopeless."

Mary guided Martin back to his chair, rewarded him with a naked cup of tea.

"Here and now, no, there ain't a thing we can do. But, just maybe, if we take a journey, then maybe we can. It's dangerous mind, dangerous to you especially, because you know damn well it's a trap." She said whilst handing Martin a tissue.

"You mean cross over. Anything but that."

"Then your daughter's dead and her soul is lost for eternity."

Her cold statement left Martin in no doubt of the result of inactivity.

"Sometimes Martin, we need to face our fears. Yours is one of the worst. You're going up against those who have lost all goodness and now only evil and spite dwell in their hearts. The Abiku want nothing but your destruction, eat you alive, tear you apart, limb from limb. They'll feast on your beating heart, rip your brain from your skull and devour every memory you've ever had."

She garnered no pleasure from her dark words.

"They want you, Martin. Maybe then their chief will release your daughter or maybe he won't. I cannot say, but you and me both know you can't just leave things be."

Martin agreed.

"So what do we do when we get there? Will you be close by? Won't you get hurt?"

"Only if I let them hurt me, and I don't intend to. They respect me, yet they know I can't go and get your daughter out. I can help you find her, but Martin, you must get her out yourself and believe in the power of light. For when you are at your lowest point, that is the time to call out to the light and maybe, just maybe, if your lucks in, things will change. Maybe then, the Abiku will be the ones who do the running."

Martin drained his cup. He paid no heed to the heat of the liquid for his spirit was cold. Mary took the cup from him, led him to the stairs.

"Where we go Martin, is a place of immense danger. You know this already for you've already been there. You will see things, some good but almost all are bad. Just remember why you are going, remember that."

Martin followed his guide up a flight of stairs decorated by a thinning grey carpet in silence. Three children atop of the stairs scampered at the sight of their mother.

"Now don't come and disturb me. No-one is to come inside my room, understand?"

The children led by Patrick bobbed their heads in terror. Martin knew she was not a woman to be tampered with despite her pleasing manner.

"Close the door behind you and flick the lock, just in case Patrick decides to get curious."

The room in total darkness yielded with reluctance to the miniature sun coming to life. Martin closed the door and secured two bolts. The room empty but for a table, two wicker chairs and a strange chart atop the table cloth.

"Please sit down, close your eyes. Don't pay too much heed to the weird writing you see. It's my own Ouija board, it will help us on our journey."

He heard the chair opposite crackle under her slender weight. She grasped his hands with tender fingers. His skin tingled and electricity hummed around them both.

Mary Celestial chanted in her native tongue. He did not understand any of it yet drifted into deep relaxation.

They both rose, hovered above the small block of Peabody flats and floated ever higher. They looked down to see London become England, England to the United Kingdom, then to Europe and the world. Ever further did Mary take him and now the world seemed tiny, a mere speck in the celestial playground. Still further they fled until at last they landed on a surface, alien, barren and foreboding.

"You know where we are, Martin?" she whispered.

Painful memories surged back. He recalled the terror of being eaten alive.

"The edge of hell?"

Mary eased herself to a wall rising higher than the roof of the universe. A dark hole gaped open to Martin's left, daring him to enter.

"It's time, my friend. Be brave, but don't give in to hate."

The medium shouted out the name of Kelly Lowe. The hole widened ever further. A golden carpet unfurled from the strange portal inviting him to enter.

"No. Not yet. Not until we know where to go."

Mary stood, covered in dark light. Her black skin blazed gold from the heat of her warm soul. She moved to the edge of the void, screaming out the words Kelly Lowe.

"Martin? Is that you?"

Mary stopped her incantation. A black youth, handsome talented but dead for a good score of years shuffled towards an old friend.

"Has it been so long? We used to have such fun."

Martin struggled to speak. His voice succumbed to dreadful shock.

"Remember how we used to hang out? We were the best of mates weren't we?"

"Johnny? It can't be."

"Look at you. You're all grown up and you've a family too. Stacey, yeah, she was good, I'm glad you got together."

Mary sidled to her passenger's side in silence.

"God I've missed you. We should have grown up together, we should have been friends for life until those bastards took you away."

He wilted under the memory of when his friend departed his life forever.

"Ah well, shit happens, Mart. I'm kind of enjoying it here, but take a tip from me and get away from these parts. You don't want to go in there."

The spirit of Johnny pointed to the dark portal, shaking his head.

"You can't go in there, Mart. You go in and you don't come back, them's the rules."

A fiery chill emanated from the darkness. Martin peered into the void and made out the shape of a creature shuffling towards him.

"He has no choice, child. But it's good of you to try and warn him. You have a good heart."

Johnny looked at the impressive medium and shielded his eyes. Her radiance dazzled in this new plain.

"You're here to help him? You going in there as well?"

Martin glanced to Mary expecting her to nod.

"No. I cannot go in. I can only show him the way."

The creature in the darkness became more prevalent. Its back bent, its presence powerful, its manner spiteful.

"You want to see your daughter then?" it croaked.

The voice rasping, scornful. The cloak of radiance surrounding Mary glimmered for a moment, darting away from the potent creature inside.

"I'm going to have to go, Martin. It's a bit too dangerous for me here. I don't like him much." said Johnny.

Johnny offered his spirit hand to Martin's and they embraced.

"I don't like you much either, sprog. What's it like to be murdered eh? Painful as fuck for a little prick like you."

Johnny fled. The creature roared with laughter, yet stayed in his domain.

"That's not very nice. I mean, how can a mere shadow of a human have the nerve to speak to him so."

Mary's radiance switched onto an incredible intensity. The hunchback shielded his eyes and shuffled back.

"What's this, Marty? You got another black one with you? I bet your wife is a dark as well? Although, no she isn't? I mean, I've seen your daughter after all and she's as white as can be. You should see how sweet and juicy she is."

Martin, eager to plant his fist on the beast's jaw crossed dangerously close to the threshold.

"Hush up, you spiteful little wretch. Take your bullshit back to your papa, foul Abiku." said Mary.

The demon backed away a few paces. Mary placed her hand on Martin's shoulder allowing her light to banish the animus within.

"Oh, so, so righteous and radiant, isn't she, little Mary?"

The hunchback ascended the tunnel once more, his form bigger, straighter.

"No, go away from me."

"So righteous when she left her baby alone. You remember back home, don't you?"

Mary slumped forward and Martin caught her.

"Fancy leaving him so you could go to your sister's party. Fancy leaving him in the care of worthless old Franklyn, a drunk, a lush and a soul of our very own."

Mary resurrected long forgotten memories. Her radiance dimmed to a dull orange hue.

"Look at me now, Mary Songo. Look at me now and see what I have."

She faced her tormentor. He stood naked except for an all too small loincloth. Below his throat lay a necklace full of bleached bones. The ogre tore one off and it sparked into life in his giant paw.

"No, go away from me. Get back to hell."

He ignored her, and caressed the small ball of what seemed to be clay in his hand.

"Look now at your precious Celestine, whore of a mother. Look now at the gift you gave to the Abiku."

Martin, horrified, stared into the eyes of a child no older than six months. A monstrous scream rent the air from the tunnel and enveloped Martin's guide. The baby's curly hair flickered with undead electricity and the owner dangled the infant in front of him, shaking it to and fro.

"You were so generous, Mary. What a precious gift you gave to us."

The giant prodded the babies ear. The screaming increased and the eyes widened ever further. The whites of the eyes darkened with red, its lips open with fanged milk teeth and its voice screamed 'Mama.'

Martin looked at Mary who cowered before her son. Never-ending tears streamed down her face at the unwanted renewal of a long-stored grief. She beat her fists on the ground and the beast continued to taunt her.

"It was your unworthy mother who is at fault. It is you who should come here and be with your son. You should be the one who shares his fate and punishment."

He delivered the rant with diabolical fervour. The baby's teeth glistened with malice and the pallor of his skin darkened with ill-intent. The babies ossified features contorted with abandonment and hatred for his mother who left him to die.

"Mary, young Celestine suffered terribly at our hands. We poked him, we skewered him, we gouged him, skinned him and devoured him."

The medium straightened herself and looked towards the Abiku's eyes, ignoring the torment of her son.

"Foul creature that you are, I have no need of you but I am not what you seek, am I?"

Mary bathed herself in divine light once more. The creature, retreated at her return to grace threw the screaming fetish aside, before returning to the hideous hunchback of before.

"Shame though Mary, you know we would make you at home in here, still, you are right, we both know why I have really come."

The hunchback pointed at Martin.

"You want your daughter back, don't you? Do you want to make a deal?"

Martin stumbled, terrified of accepting the hunchback's offer.

"Martin, remember, believe in yourself and the gift within you. Do what you must, accept your decision and go and get your child."

The hunchback offered his hand, daring Martin to accept.

"Kelly's quite at home, you know, she's being well looked after. And Martin, it really isn't so bad you know, after all you've been here before haven't you?"

He stepped ever closer to the gangrenous sweaty hand before him.

"Yes, go on, take my hand and follow. Leave your precious guide behind."

The beast's face etched in triumph when it accepted Martin's palm. Mary Celestial remained motionless, unable to follow.

"Martin, remember who you are, don't lose that fact no matter what they do to you and Kelly. And remember one last thing."

He looked round one last time before the sepulchral darkness consumed him.

"When you are at your lowest, that is the time to ask. That it is the time."

He did not understand. The hunchback sealed the tunnel and led him in, down, down, down into the darkest places of imagination. Down to be with his daughter again.

Chapter 26 Confrontation

His every step on descent invited destruction from any moment. Martin and his unusual companion bathed in a peculiar orange hue from a sole source of illumination above, almost like a parody of the dog star. The hunchback dashed with surprising speed, urging Martin to keep up.

"Nice to be back, isn't it, Mart? Things have changed a bit, but not too much, you know. I'm sure you'll recognise a few familiar sights."

Martin scanned ahead and the hunchback's face shimmered before him. Instead of whiskers, he sported sugar, his eyes transformed into a pair of caramelised orbs and a pair of shortbread fangs offered a savage grin. He paused before the hunchback dismissed the illusion.

"Good to see you haven't forgotten your last trip here. Those biscuits were quite the rage back then."

The creature seized Martin's wrist, urging him ever down.

"Who are you? What are you?"

They rounded a small corner, the stairs yielded to a ramp.

"Why that's jolly nice of you to ask, Marty. Seeing as you're here it can't do no harm to tell you. My name, well, let's not overcomplicate things. Just call me Harry and I've been around for, hmm, about as long as your planet, I suppose."

A noxious fragrance whirled around the pair with each passing step.

"As for what I am. Well, the dizzy medium said I'm one of the Abiku. I suppose a fair reflection in an odd kind of way but quite irrelevant to you, my Cockney Sparrow. Just call me a shadow fiend. I think that'll do for now."

Martin's gaze squinted to fathom the end of the ever spiralling ramp, each step, deeper than the last.

"Us fiends are pretty decent once you get to know us. Those clowns from the other side put us in a bad light, not fair at all, really."

Martin didn't believe a word.

"What about my daughter? What about the time you tried to take me before? Why did you try and take us?"

The hunchback stopped, affronted by the accusation. With mock shock, it placed its hand across its chest.

"Oh Martin, that really is most unfair. We didn't kidnap anyone, both you and your daughter's actions brought you both here. You tripped over and Kelly fucked around with Ouija boards. You really can't put the blame on us, you invited yourself."

Martin tried to argue yet no coherent words escaped. Harry the hunchback nodded, satisfied his captive understood.

"You see don't you? You can't screw around with us. You ask for attention and we gladly give it."

The ramp ended and led to a concrete path dissecting a set of flats. Martin baulked at the familiar yet alien surroundings. His own block of flats, a wicked parody of his own abode with a slate grey sky threatening crimson rain.

Jeers and catcalls escaped from a group of youths, feral, dark with malice. They left the haven of a ground floor flat and paced towards the two strangers.

"It's all right boys, the governor knows all about Martin's little journey."

The teenagers ignored Harry's words. Desperate to relieve their boredom, one of the group reached inside a jacket of hide.

"We're looking for fun now. He's lost and far from home, ain't he? Let me just give him a memento."

The youth's flick-knife arrowed towards Martin's throat. Martin stumbled and lost his balance. The boy missed, then kicked Martin's stomach. Harry, enraged, took command.

"You useless little gits. Didn't I tell you he's here under the governor's orders?"

Harry's hands transformed into claws. He slapped Martin's attacker and the youth flew across the courtyard and smashed into someone's front window, covering the glass with black blood.

"You want some as well, do you? Come on then, if you think you're hard enough."

The remaining gang members shied away. Harry reached down, brushed the sooty earth away from Martin.

"Sorry about that, Marty. These young ones can be a bit boisterous. Still, a little slap always seems to be just the ticket."

Martin thanked his guide. Harry, amused at the unexpected gratitude, pointed at the third floor balcony.

"Look familiar? It should do Marty, after all, this is your daughter's creation."

Martin looked at the same place they lived in, the same stairs, the same glass fronted balconies, the same stench of human detritus he knew so well. Martin even fumbled in his pockets.

"Ha-ha, don't be silly, mate. I know it looks the same, but your key won't work. Let's go and say hello to your Kelly, shall we?"

Martin sped ahead of Harry, relieved at the thought of seeing his daughter. He sprinted to the lime coated doors before looking at the different numbers upon the intercom.

"Well go on, they won't let you in unless you ask."

Martin pressed the buttons and almost at once a strange voice, not unlike his own answered.

"Hello? What'd you want?"

Harry indicated for Martin to speak.

"I want to see my daughter. Is she in there?"

Cold laughter echoed back.

"Martin, it must be Martin. Good to hear your voice, mate."

"Is my daughter in there?" he spat.

The intercom fell silent and the door buzzed. Martin climbed the stairs and seized command of his rising nausea.

"Ah, there's nothing like a friendly family re-union is there? This all gives me a bit of tear in me eye."

Martin paid Harry no heed. He shoved aside a wizened drunk and edged ever closer to his caged daughter, determined to beat the crap out of her surrogate family.

"Go on Martin. Get up them stairs and give them a good hiding. It's what they deserve, after all. They need a good slap."

Harry's words galvanised Martin to heightened fury. The door to the flat lay open. Martin burst inside. Harry giggled in ecstasy when he heard blows being exchanged and someone fall to the floor. Harry pushed his way inside to find Martin prostrate with three heavy figures kicking and punching his unprotected body.

"Oh Martin, I thought you'd at least say hello before sticking the boot in. Don't you know wraith families are way stronger than you can imagine?"

Martin lapsed into black silence. His lips lay covered with a stream of sticky blood. His breathing struggled under the rage of Kelly's adopted parents.

"That's really not friendly of you to come wandering over here, looking for a bit of 'agg. Here have some of that."

Kelly's shadow parent landed a punch on his cheek. A tooth flew across the passageway.

"All right, all right that'll do people."

Martin's double switched on the flickering hallway light. His lips twisted with globules of gangrenous saliva, hair greased in blue gel and his face pock-marked by angry long dead sores.

"OK, Harry, you sure we can't give him a bit more of a battering? I want to stamp on the twat's skull a bit more."

Martin's double grabbed him hard by the lapels of his jacket, hurling him upright.

"No, he's got an appointment to see his daughter. We've got to have him at least looking a bit half decent."

The shadow, disappointed slunk away to his son and wife.

"Where is she? Where is Kelly? You said she'd be here."

Harry admired Martin's sudden surge of strength.

"Did I? I think you're mistaken. No, I just wanted you to say hello to her family, that's all. I mean, if my daughter was being cared for, I'd want to know she was in good hands."

The watching trio burst out into spontaneous glee. Their dark mouths filled with a glaze of white enamel, their skulls bobbed in sadistic mirth.

"You bastards. You call this care?"

"We're all bastards, Martin. Not as much as the bastard who gave her life though. What a nob he is. Ponces around at work, let's his daughter muck about with the occult and all that bollocks. I mean, you'd have thought he'd have learned after all what he has been though."

Martin's rage swirled again. Harry admired his animus.

"What's she ever done to you? Take me to her."

Harry grabbed the side of Martin's head and twisted the stump of hair and pulled his ear towards his mouth.

"Not just yet. Anyway, it was you who sent her to us. Your neglect ensured her passage. All we had to do was wait. Now she's ours."

"No, not yours. Never. Let her go."

Harry shook his head.

"It's not down to me. That's down to the chief. His word is law. He'll take some convincing to be deprived of his new little pet."

"So take me to him. I don't know why you ever brought me here."

Harry looked away disappointed.

"That's a nice way to talk about Kelly's guardians. Anyway, you never know Martin, the boss might make them look after you. It depends on how things go."

Harry's eyes shifted from red to dead yellow. He nudged his head towards the door.

"Come on Martin, time to scoot."

Harry thanked Kelly's adopted parents and shepherded his bleeding charge towards the lift. The lift took them back to the courtyard.

"You look a bit of a state. Here, let's fix you up a tad."

Harry took out a handkerchief and dabbed away the globules of blood across his shattered lip. He didn't bother with the ribs; they weren't necessary to be on show during the 'interview.'

"So where do we go now then?"

"Have a wander that's what. Oh, for fuck's sake."

Harry scowled at the group of youths watching from near the edge of the block of flats.

"I told you lot to scram. I ain't going to tell you again."

The youths backed away. All except one. The one who dared to be brave earlier on.

"You're not so hard, Mister. You just got lucky."

The wannabe devil didn't bother trying to maintain his human form any more. A wretch wreathed in hardened black skin sprinted straight at Harry.

"Stupid as well as wild. Oh well, I'm starving anyway."

The youth lashed out at the starving demon with a taloned strike. The attack made no impression on Harry's formidable armoured skin. He seized the suicidal boy by the neck and bit down. The attacker's curses stuck in its jugular. Harry snapped his jaws together and tore the head from its previous owner. Martin's legs buckled at the display of supreme savagery. Harry, the smiling carouser, transformed into his true bestial nature, an example of supreme evil.

The demon tore the body in half. He stuffed everything into his gaping mouth, legs, genitalia, chest, arms and all the rest.

"Boy, did I need that. I can't tell you how bad that makes my stomach turn, Mart. Imagine a place where all you can taste is the reek of rotting flesh, dried old spunk and shit and that's what he tastes like. Still, fills a hole though."

Harry returned to his original form. The tattered suit he wore flapped in the gulf stream of a satanic breeze.

"Thanks, I didn't need the gory details though."

"Ha-ha, well not everything tastes as rotten as demon flesh. We do have some lovely grub from time to time."

Martin dared not ask what.

"Scared to ask? Can't say as I blame you but you know what the sweetest thing of all to eat is down here?"

"I shudder to think."

"That's the spirit. The sweetest thing of all down here is innocent flesh. You know, a sprog gone bad. The flesh of them little suckers is the best thing a demon could ever eat. Trouble is, it's down to the governor where they go."

Harry's malevolent eyes glazed over in remembrance of a long forgotten feast.

"It's been a while since I had a one of them on a spit. Still, you never know when I might get a delicious surprise."

He led Martin into an abandoned small alley. Martin's eyes focused on one word standing proud in green neon: Entrance.

"Here we go, Mart. I have to tell you, behave yourself in there. The main man doesn't take kindly to people who don't show respect. You piss him off and then God help you… Well, he would if he could."

A door in blood black awaited. Harry nudged the wood open. He guided Martin down a passage where walls glistened in waspish venom. Several eerie red parcels lay stacked six boxes high and two deep.

"Devoured old souls, in case you're wondering. We've sucked all the goodness out and we're waiting for a collection. You punters are so easy to corrupt, it's unbelievable. Come on, it's down here, Martin."

Martin's insides churned over and over. He followed his escort, down, always down to a pale blue light.

"This is as far as I go. The rest is up to you, your daughter and the governor. Remember, treat him right and you might get your way, I doubt it though."

Martin's eyes swam in a universe of cerulean lasers. He heard a door slam behind and at last beheld the originator of his sufferance. A man, small, suited and offering an amicable smile urged him to step forward.

Chapter 27 Bargain Basement

Martin scoured his surroundings. The marble floor showered blue light from its veins. Beside him great tomes teetered in a precarious fashion from mahogany bookcases enticing the reader with ancient wisdom. His senses swam with the scent of fresh coffee and a hint of mint. At the end of a strip of red carpet, his host waited in magnificent patience.

The bald host wore a yellow suit, his shirt white, tie kippered and a wreath of curbed gold lay across his neck. His shoes shone so bright Martin witnessed his own reflection

"Ah, Martin, Martin, Martin, I cannot say how much I've been looking forward to this moment. Come on in, come on in."

The man's accent strong of Bermondsey. His grip immense when he took possession of Martin's hand within his own.

"It's so good to see you, really good. Coffee OK or do you fancy something stronger? I've all sorts of poison in here, mate."

Martin's voice failed. He searched his thoughts, looking for signs of what to say.

"Well speak up. I can't have you going mute on me. Oh I get it, you're expecting all brimstone and fire, ain't you? Mate, that went out way back in the middle ages. Things have moved on, we're a bit more professional these days."

"Could I have a cup of tea?" croaked Martin.

The host nodded with enthusiasm. He groped for a slim green phone and hammered a few keys.

"All right Trev, rustle up a cup of Rosie. How many sugars, Mart?"

"Just the one."

"One sugar and make sure you bring up some biscuits, as well."

The businessman indicated for Martin to take a seat.

"Sorry, but where is my daughter?"

The man said nothing, instead he reached into a weathered Bisley and searched for 'K.' He brought out an orange file marked 'New.'

"Straight to business then. I mean there's no point in fart-arsing about, is there?"

Impatient fingers prised open the file. Martin focused on Kelly staring back in grim obedience. Her picture fresh, her image sharp.

"There you go, all safe and sound in my own personal chambers. She's quite a girl."

Martin gazed into eyes of diabolical triumph. The beast held a supreme sense of smugness, indifference and victory. Martin's despair burst forth in a spectacular eruption of total fury.

"What have you done? What the fuck do you want?"

He grabbed the man by his jacket and shoved him hard against the filing cabinet.

"Hmm, rage, what a splendid display of anger you possess."

"You better tell me where she is or I'll fucking kill you. Where is she?"

The suited man smiled back.

"You'll kill me? Really? Martin, forgive me but you're way out of your league. Don't you know who you're fucking with?"

Martin's palms backed away from the intense heat flowing from the jacket. Flames danced around the host's head who remained silent and pointed at the empty chair.

"The devil? Are you the devil?"

The stranger remained quiet, took his seat and stared into Martin's tender soul.

"Good lord no. He's far too busy to waste his time on a little prick like you. No, I'm just what would you call me? One of his helpers, I suppose. Not exactly one of the princes of hell but far, far up above a little scroat like you."

A white panel swung open, a shadow wraith entered and padded towards its master with a tray containing two china cups and a red carton marked 'assorted.'

"Hello Trev, you've met Martin before, haven't you?"

The shadow's red eyes flickered in fond remembrance. It flicked open the lid for its employer. "Yes Mr. Brown. We know each other very well."

Mr. Brown offered his guest a selection of biscuits. To Martin's dismay, the biscuits growled at his touch, their faces armed with the cruel fangs he remembered from long ago.

"I see you remember my little friends. Go on, you can bite their heads off, they won't mind at all."

Mr. Brown ordered Trev away and dipped a shortbread into his coffee before decapitating the offending snack.

"I call 'em hotbites, pretty apt, don't you think?"

Martin tickled a pink wafer. Its black eyes dared him to follow the lead of the high demon sitting opposite.

"Go on, just stick it in your cuppa. They're not quite so bolshy when they're wet."

Martin obeyed without a second look. He looked into Mr. Brown's blue eyes, stuck the biscuit in his mouth and chewed. "Pretty good, eh?"

Martin agreed.

"Well, I stuck a lot of that magic go-go juice you used to dabble in back in the day into my biccies. You should never have gone clean, you know, it made my job so much harder."

The world changed. Before him now stood not the pleasant face of Mr. Brown but a great beast, eyes ancient, its expression cruel, victorious. It sat quite naked and a black aura glowered in power. The marble vanished and they sat in a pitch dark room illuminated by a solitary dangling orange bulb. His bones froze and he stomped his feet. Martin stood naked and he read the lascivious intent within the beast.

Mr. Brown brought Martin's face so close he could taste the stench of the demon's breath.

"Lucky for you I'm not in the mood for love just now. Me and you have got other things to talk about. Down to business, down to the nitty gritty. How much do you want your daughter?"

"She's everything to me. Just give her back."

Mr. Brown slapped Martin across the face. His blow sent Martin to the floor. Martin shoulder's skin tore away when the demon brought his face towards his own.

"Answer the frigging question, you dozy prick. How much do you want your daughter? What are you going to do, to make me let her go?"

"Whatever it takes. Whatever you want."

Martin's soul fell. He readied himself for damnation.

"Are you sure about that mate? There's no going back. You make the deal and your arse is mine for the whole of bloody eternity."

"But she goes free?"

Mr. Brown nodded. A piece of grey parchment descended next to Martin's foot.

"You ready to sign?"

"Yeah, you got a pen?"

"This is hell, you don't need a poxy pen."

Mr. Brown grabbed Martin's forearm and bit. Spectral blood dripped towards his wrist.

"Sign. Sign it now."

Martin never bothered to read the satanic covenant. His blood fell, fell to a solitary square box. At once the blackness shrivelled to a haze of red. His eyes settled on a cage beside Mr. Brown. The cage contained his abducted daughter. Beside it, lay a new cage, man sized and with a halter and array of chains.

"Let her go."

"Get in dog. Get in and put them on."

Shadow wraiths poured into the chamber. Their clawed hands nipped and probed their new inmate. His neck choked when fresh metal bit, the steel ripped into his ankles and wrists. He huddled to the tiny cage's entrance.

The shadow's pushed. His head snapped at a ludicrous angle in the confines of the cage, he could not move yet they grabbed his ankles and pushed. Scrabbling hands nipped at his testicles and buttocks and shoved. At last, inside, captured and at his new lord's mercy.

Mr. Brown shuffled forward and gripped a handle atop Martin's new metal home. He hoisted the cage and walked to a wall of grey where to Martin's horror he witnessed a rack of similar cages. The inhabitants yelled in endless protest yet none paid heed in the human kennel.

"My daughter. Is she free yet?"

Mr. Brown ignored the question. He traced a path to the letter 'L' and slotted his new visitor next to a gremlin of a human and an empty space. Martin assumed it was his liberated daughter.

"You should have read the small print. I'll be back in a sec."

His brow narrowed into conduits of concern. The bars tore their sadistic trace into his cheeks and his tongue drooled feral saliva. His new master returned carrying a cage.

"No, you promised. You said she can go. We've got a deal."

Mr. Brown shoved Kelly's home next to Martin. Martin screamed in disbelief.

"Let her go."

Mr. Brown licked his lips before turning to Martin.

"We do have a deal. She will be free but I didn't say right away, did I? How old does she have to be? Ah, that's it, seventy five and then she's released. Not like you, you're mine for eternity."

His daughter twisted her head to face her dad. Her molten tears streamed in endless hopelessness mirroring her father.

"Daddy? I'm so sorry, Daddy."

His daughter's apology so vacant.

"It's all right babe, it's not your fault. It'll be fine, don't worry."

Martin's promise was too much for Mr. Brown. His voice boomed in derision.

"Of course it'll be fine, Kel. You know the drill, you do what I tell you and remember how bad a girl you've been. Still, don't worry, I've arranged for your Mummy and Daddy to pick you up soon. Their son really misses you."

"You tricked me. You know what I meant, you know what I fucking meant," screamed Martin.

"It's not my fault you're thick. It's not that hard to read and write. Do yourself a favour and get used to it."

Martin cried, cried for the fact he couldn't help his daughter, cried for the fact he had no hope, cried for the fact he failed as a father. He begged to die.

"Die? You want to die? Hard lines, you're not going anywhere."

Martin's mind claimed a recent memory, recent, yet it seemed so long ago.

"When you see no path, ask for help. Ask for help and don't give in too hate. You can find a way for both you and your daughter." Mary's voice, a breath of heaven. The demon stirred, annoyed at something unseen intruding upon his dominion.

"What's that? Some soppy moo trying to make contact, is she? Well tell her from me the slag's wasting her precious time."

Kelly shrank under the torrent from the beast. She remembered his cruelty when enraged.

"Help me Mary, please help free me and my daughter."

"Get out. Get your filthy stinking arse out of my home or I swear I'll drag you down here to join your son on Harry's neck. How'd you like me to rip the soul out your so righteous body and tie you down. You know what'll happen if I catch you here."

"Don't ask me, Martin, I can't do what you ask. You've got think bigger, much bigger and bolder."

Martin's reverie shattered when Mr. Brown smashed his fist onto the cage's side. His left finger broke yet no pain came. All Martin thought of was a figure blessed in white, protective and strong, so unbelievably strong."

"God, angel or whoever you are, please I beg you, help me, help my daughter."

Mr. Brown howled. He grabbed Martin's cage and hurled it with all his force across the room.

"You shouldn't have said that. You stupid witless prick. I'm so going to make you suffer, make you both suffer."

The door to the cage opened under the impact. Mr. Brown grabbed Martin's ankle and dragged out his victim. He threw him onto a table, face down, ready to be punished.

"I'm going to abuse you Again, again, again and again. Fucking angels, I ain't having that, no way."

Mr. Brown forced Martin's arms high up on the huge desk. He writhed when the demon lowered himself and found his way inside. The demon's captive clasped his hands together and imagined what his protector would look like.

He expected the demon to thrust and hurt him. He instead glanced ahead and discovered his hands were glowing. He sensed no pain, only contentment and intense happiness. He witnessed a form develop from the energy pouring out of his hands. He heard a scream behind him calling for aid.

"You're not welcome, sod off or I'll beat the shit out of you as well."

Martin's newcomer took on a human form and become more defined with each passing second.

"Now, now, that's no way to speak to one of us, is it? I mean, it doesn't take much to be civil, does it?"

"Piss off."

The radiance vanished from Martin's guest. He wore no white garb or heavenly robes. He wore an England top, a pair of dirty jeans and steel toe capped boots. Upon his right wrist lay a heavy gold bracelet and all his fingers were adorned with rings. Both fists spelt out the promise 'have that.' His right hand held a bar of iron and he tapped the weapon upon his left palm.

"Hello Martin, Charlie at your service mate, Lady Nel said I should keep an eye out for you. Now let's sort this clown out and get you out of here."

Mr. Brown shied away from the golden light from his unwelcome visitor.

"You shouldn't have come here. You're far from home and outmatched."

The shadow demon placed his fingers in his mouth and blew three hard shrill blasts. Mr. Brown's associates filled the chamber. First was Trev, eyes feral, fearful but determined. He licked his lips at the thought of gnawing upon pure flesh. Harry stood next to him and hordes of shadow fiends joined the throng along with stunted walking biscuits, armed with chocolate cleavers. Their button-holed eyes seeing nothing but black death for their radiant opponent. Kelly's foster parents were the last to enter. Her mother armed with a rolling pin decorated with a fistful of nails, her husband sported a snooker cue and their wastrel of a son brandished a tiny dagger.

"Like I said, you should never have come."

Charlie said nothing to Mr. Brown. He laid his hands on Martin's shoulders, dismissing his guilt, his pain, rage and fear. He looked to Kelly who shivered in the tiny confines of her cage and the bars wilted and faded away. He beckoned the confused child towards her father. She ran, invisible to her tormentors who shied away from the yellow mantle about her shoulders.

Mr. Brown witnessed her flight. He yelled in disgust at his charges blindness.

"Fools. They're getting away, attack. Attack now and kill the fucker."

Martin went to the Charlie's side determined to fight.

"No my friend. Your battle is over. It's down to me to sort this out."

The shadow fiends launched the first assault. Bile splattered claws enshrouded in darkness leapt upon the intruder who remained impassive when they fell upon him. Martin fled from the growing ball of impenetrable black. His hopes faltered, terrified his saviour had been devoured. A gentle voice gusted through his despairing thoughts.

"*Be at peace. They cannot win.*" Said Mary.

Martin spotted a dot of yellow in the midst of darkness. It grew to the size of a football and at once exploded in glory. The wraiths disintegrated under the tremendous blaze. Charlie stood, a confident smile etched across his wondrous face.

"I've just about had enough of this old bollocks."

Charlie grabbed hold Trev by his tail and dragged the cowering devil towards him.

"What's the matter mate, lost your bottle?"

He swung his crowbar across the wraith's neck, severing head from torso. He plunged his hand into the beast's shivering body and ripped out its black heart.

"Another one bites the dust," he sung in delight.

Kelly's shadow brother attacked next. Charlie broke his neck with a flick of his wrist. He repelled the father with a kick to the knee, an elbow to the ribs and a head-butt. Martin's twisted facsimile protested with a broken nose. Charlie silenced him when a crowbar smashed into his chest and skewered his heart.

"Ah, what fun. I do love a tear up. Who's up next?"

A corrupted Stacey glared at him. Not with fear but absolute loathing for the destruction of her family. She swung her rolling pin at his head.

He caught her blow with his right hand, the force breaking his assailant's arm. She remained where she was, unable to move. Charlie threw away the pin and grabbed her wrist and pushed her to the ground. With his hand still about her arm he traced his left towards her opposite ankle and yanked her to her feet.

She screamed a terrible dirge. The curses of what she wanted to do to Kelly and her father stung the air and forced Martin's daughter to shrivel in dread.

"You really are a bitter old mare, aren't you? Now do us all a favour and shut your trap."

He pulled the adopted mother's body apart with divine power. Rotten offal showered the room with her dying remains before Charlie ripped out her organ of life.

"Now there are two. Well come on then, you want some or what?"

Mr. Brown ordered Harry to advance. The pot-bellied giant reached to his neck and unclasped a necklace. He set Mary's baby to the ground and the toddler darted towards Charlie, eager to feed. It raced up his sleeve and its teeth found the expanse of his neck.

He did not bleed. The baby backed away, fresh life animating its dark face. The cruel grey of torment left the infant and Charlie scooped the child into his arms.

"You are free now, my beautiful child. Free to go home and far, far from here."

The child took the honey of joy and laughed for the first time in its new life. The enforcer clapped his hands and the baby flew upon downy wings. It soared away and Harry bellowed in rage.

Mary Celestial's voice sang a word of blissful thanks.

"No. That fetish was mine. I'm not going to have that. Never."

Mr. Brown united with his fell colleague. They circled Charlie, desperate for blood.

"All right, time to get this sorted."

Mr. Brown struck first, his claws ripping across Charlie's cheek sending his golden fluid across the room. Harry launched himself into his torso, causing them both to fall. The angel did not stir and both Harry and Mr. Brown set about the task of destruction.

Martin, despite the folly, ran behind Mr. Brown and punched him hard in the small of the back.

"Are you some sort of cunt?"

The demon swivelled in one move and grabbed his attacker by the neck and drew him to his face.

"You're taking the piss, Martin. Fucking hell, am I going to make you pay. Your mate couldn't save you from me, nothing can."

Martin heard Harry continue his assault. Blow after blow rained into Charlie's prostrate form. Yet, despite this a sonorous voice rang clear.

"Martin, Martin, Martin, I told you your part in the fighting is over. This is between me and these two tossers now."

A swirl of a fat man flew across the room, his chest punctured and heart missing. Charlie seized Mr. Brown's arm and broke it in one easy movement. Martin dropped to the ground.

"God, oops sorry boss, I wish I could rip your poxy heart out and end your miserable life, you moody sod. I'd have to drag you all the way home to do that though, and to be honest I can't be arsed."

Mr. Brown swung his other fist into Charlie's face, forcing him to wince. His grip remained firm.

"I'm going to bury you son. Right here on your home patch. Right here in Marty's weird world."

The demon's eyes flushed from yellow to blue with bright fear redolent in its veins.

"No. I will never suffer it, my master will not allow it."

"Your master can't be bothered with a little shit like you. Face it, you're done."

Charlie glanced towards the former captives and pointed to the left.

"There you go, your own little stairway to heaven. Now hurry up on there because this whole place is coming down. Go on, pull your finger out."

The two escapees needed no prompting. They dashed towards a cerulean balustrade escalator and floated away back to the beautiful light.

Martin glanced down. A tremendous sound of falling rubble and dust blasted out far below and he heard Mr. Brown being entombed. The demon screamed out one last time, before silence claimed his voice. Below, a glyph of the sun bound the creature in his eternal prison.

Martin's soul pulsed with pure joy. He spotted a blaze of gold rise. Its light warm, encompassing and briefly settled before father and daughter.

"Now you two, get back home and don't let me see you until you're a lot older. Now bloody well look after yourselves."

Martin smiled a thank you.

"Oh, and Martin, don't turn your back on your 'gift'. I don't just give them out willy nilly. You ought to be doing more than just delivering parcels. Have a word with Mary when you get back home. She'll help you."

His fear of his calling vanished at Charlie's address. He embraced his daughter, pulling her close with all his might.

"Thank you, Charlie. God bless you."

The angel laughed.

"He already has, you sop. Now go on, get back home, 'cause I'm out of here."

The air around them shone in brilliant white. He no longer held his daughter when his eyes adjusted to another place. He blinked twice and saw a beautiful woman smiling at the joy of her dead son's liberation.

"Well Martin, I think we need to go the hospital, don't you?"

Chapter 28 Always

Mum's round again. She gets so lonely these days. Still, she always brightens up when Tony sees his Nan. Four years old the little squirt is now. I can't complain though. I mean, ever since Dad saved me. How long is it now? Fuck me, yeah fourteen years ago. I'll always remember what he did for me, always. Tony, he's only gone and splattered ice cream over his mush.

"You're supposed to eat it."

He's laughing and scraping it up onto his fingers and stuffing it into his mouth. Mum's fussing as ever with her tissue and telling him to stop.

"Kel, you ought to teach Tone how to eat proper."

"He's getting there, Mum."

Off she goes to the kitchen. Spoiling the little git with more ice cream, no doubt. Oh well, mustn't complain really. I mean, Tony's father's a real diamond, good as gold. I got lucky 'cause a lot of the pricks round here ain't worth a wank, but my Del, I wouldn't swap him for the world. He never moans, always has a smile on his face and looks after us. Oh, and I still fancy him something rotten.

"There, that's better. Now you show your Nan how to eat your ice cream properly."

Can't believe he'll be at school soon. Where do the years go eh? I mean look at me, twenty-nine. It's been two years since Dad went away. I can see him in my boy though. Same little laugh and the same blue eyes.

Is that the time? I better get the grub on 'cause Del will be home soon. Mum's at my side as ever, helping me get it all sussed. She's a proper Gordon Ramsey when it comes to cooking, and there's five of us at the table 'cause my brother's coming over with his bird.

"Six, you dopey mare. Can't you count?"

"Sorry Mum, I never was much cop at maths."

It'll be good for us to be all together though. We don't do it enough. I wish we did it more in the past. I really wish we did.

What the hell? I can hear laughing and jumping around. Where is it?
Tony.
I'm on my feet, scampering to his room. Fucking three A.M., for God's sake and he's acting the bloody goat. For some reason though, I don't storm into his room. I wait outside and just listen, something tells me to.
"Can you do it again? You're so funny."
Who is he talking to?
"Yeah, I will, I promise. I'll look after my Mummy. She's the best Mummy in the world."
I sneak the door open. I'm looking at my son and he don't even know I'm there. Instead, he's looking at the end of the bed and right there, there's a weird green glow. I can't speak, it's like my throat is full of crushed ice.
"Do you have to go now? Can't you stay a bit longer? Oh Grandad, you're such a spoilsport. Will you be back tomorrow? That's good then."
My boy looks up and the weird light is gone.
"Mummy, why are you crying? Have I been naughty?"
I am crying. I'm happy, so, so happy. I can't wait to tell Mum, I can't bloody wait.

Printed in Great Britain
by Amazon